940626 E

D0465162

DISCARD

East Union
High School Library
Manteca, California

DEMCO

BILL

ALSO BY CHAP REAVER

Mote

A Little Bit Dead

BILL

Chap Reaver

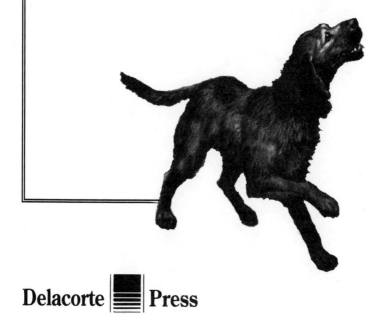

Delacorte Press

Published by
Delacorte Press
Bantam Doubleday Dell Publishing Group, Inc.
1540 Broadway
New York, New York 10036

Library of Congress Cataloging in Publication Data

Reaver, Chap.
   Bill / by Chap Reaver.
     p. cm.
   Summary: With the help of her faithful dog Bill and the officer responsible for putting her father in jail, thirteen-year-old Jessica faces changes in her life when she realizes that her father will not stop drinking and making moonshine.
   ISBN 0-385-31175-3
   [1. Dogs—Fiction. 2. Country life—Southern states—Fiction. 3. Prohibition—Fiction. 4. Southern states—Fiction.] I. Title.
PZ7.R23765Bi 1994
[Fic]—dc20   93-35491 CIP AC

Manufactured in the United States of America

May 1994

10 9 8 7 6 5 4 3 2 1

BVG

BILL

1

My dog Bill and I stood at the fence and watched Dad float away on the log raft. Behind him and downstream the creek flowed into the darkness of the woods and disappeared, like train tracks into a railroad tunnel. When he neared the edge of the trees Dad lifted his hand. Bill wagged his tail and I raised my hand back and we held like that until the woods took him.

I was still sweaty and breathing from the hurry-up work we had done, getting the raft loaded and pushed off before anybody came. A few minutes ago Dad and I had carried the last bag of sugar from the barn down to the creek and stepped onto the raft with it. We eased the sack down on top of the boxes of empty jars. Then Dad jumped back off the raft to get the big yellow tarp.

After he unfolded it on the grass he slung it over the load and we lashed it down tight, tossing the rope back and forth to crisscross the canvas.

Dad tied down the last corner, then straightened up and stretched with his fists at his back. "Well, I guess that's it, Jess."

"Yeah, that's it, I guess."

"I better be going."

I said, "How far is it?"

"Oh, it's a day's ride, something like that. Day and a half, maybe. Depends on how much I have to stop." He picked up the long pole he used. "Sometimes there's lots of deadfalls and blowdowns and I have to tie up and chop them clear before I can float through."

"Where do you sleep at night?"

"Right there." He pointed at the canvas. "It rains, I just crawl under that tarp, lay on the sugar bags. It gives me sweet dreams."

I looked at the sky. Heavy clouds darkened the west. I untied the line and threw it onto the tarp. The current nudged the raft away a few inches. Dad said, "I'll bring you something from town, some more books from the library, maybe a dress. You want to start wearing a dress?"

"Just make it books."

He nodded. "Anybody comes around now you just tell them I'm gone and you don't know where. And don't let them dig unless they pay their dollar first."

"I know."

2

Dad used his pole to push away. "And if Wrong Man shows up you don't tell him a thing, not anything."

"I know, Dad."

After Dad floated into the woods I stayed at the fence and kept watching where I had last seen him, with his hand raised up. Bill ranged around, nose-walking the fields and pawing at grasshoppers. He was just playing, but the grasshoppers were scared because they thought Bill was serious and they jumped as hard as they could.

Bill is a big brown fellow with several different kinds of dog mixed together in him. He smiles most of the time and is very smart. Dad said that Bill could learn to do just about anything I wanted him to if I would take the time and work with him. I guess Dad's right, but Bill's good right now just like he is so I leave him alone and he likes me fine the way I am too.

Dad always came back from his float-aways in a week or two, walking over the big hill and down toward the house with a couple of sacks. One sack always had two big bottles of store whiskey. One of the bottles had always been started. He brought books from town that Miss Pritchett at the library picked out for me and at night I would read to him and he'd drink his whiskey and cry. He cried when he was drunk even when I read funny stories to him. He was probably thinking about Mom and how bad he missed her.

That's why Dad drank so much in the first place, ''Trying to forget,'' he said.

Dad would lay in drunk and sick for three or four days and then be out of whiskey. We'd bake a cake to help him get over it. It was really just corn bread, the same kind of corn bread we ate every day, except on cake day we would bake two pones instead of one and stack the second one on top of the first.

I'm in charge of the icing part. I used cow butter and powdered sugar all mashed together with the back side of a fork with some sorghum syrup and sweet cream mixed in to get it smoothed out nice. I took lots of tastes while I worked it to make sure it was coming together right. Also because I just liked to taste of it. The icing goes in between the two pones, then all around the sides and on top.

After the cake Dad and I both worked the farm hard a couple days before he'd sadden up again about Mom and his nerves would start to get sharp. We'd drive into town and he'd buy sugar and things while I was at the library with Miss Pritchett. I read a lot of books. Then Dad would drive us back home licking his lips and the whole thing would start all over with building another raft and him floating off into the woods again.

There wasn't any use watching the creek anymore. I started up toward the house, stopping to pick up a stick for me and Bill. Bill will fetch a stick every time I throw it, drop it at my feet, and then grin up at me with eyes that say, *Please throw it again, Jess.* Most of the time I do because I like to see him run after it and he enjoys it so.

Bill will fetch a ball, too, or even a big chunk of firewood, dragging it along the ground backward and snarling. I got him to try to fetch a bale of hay once but he couldn't get his mouth around it and it was too heavy for throws anyway.

When we got to the chicken house I rared back and gave the stick a good high toss, over the roof to see if I could confuse him. Bill's so smart he caught on right away and began tearing around the corner. He stopped short and turned back to look at me. Then he looked away again and saw something that made him give that little ''burf'' and stiffen up his front legs.

I walked up to him and looked toward the house. There was a car in the yard and Wrong Man was sitting on the bumper with his cap pushed back.

2

I had asked my dad why he called him Wrong Man and he said that Wrong Man is what everybody else called him and he didn't know why. He came around every few weeks and talked with Dad but I wasn't allowed to hear any of it.

Wrong Man stayed sitting on his car bumper and watched us walk up. Bill wanted to growl and bark at him but soon as he'd start Wrong Man would snap his fingers and say, "Come here, boy. Come on," and Bill'd go to wagging and walking half curled up and ashamed. Bill's too friendly and tenderhearted to act mad at anybody for long.

Wrong Man looked right at Bill and talked to me. "You Leonard's girl?"

"Yes, sir."

"Were's he at?"

I shook my head. "I don't know."

Bill inched closer. Wrong Man held his hand out steady and Bill tried to smell of it by stretching his neck way out instead of taking one more step. Wrong Man said, "What's your name?"

"His name's Bill."

He looked up. "What's your name's what I meant."

"I'm Jess, Jess Gates. It's really Jessica, after my mother."

"Which do you like best, Jess or Jessica."

"Either one."

"Well, I want to call you by your favorite name, so you tell me which one it'll be."

"Jess is all right."

"Well, good. That's my favorite name too. Did you know that?"

"No. How would I know something like that?"

He grinned at Bill. "Jess, I need to talk to your daddy and it's important."

"He's not here."

Bill was close enough to smell of his fingers and Wrong Man said, "Yeah, Bill. Yeah, come on now."

I said, "He'll be back in a few days."

As soon as Wrong Man touched him, Bill was in his lap and turning circles and acting like a dog who had never been petted before in his whole life. He tried to lick Wrong Man's face, but he dodged him and laughed and scuffled his ears around with both hands. Bill just loves that.

Wrong Man said, "Not to brag or nothing, but dogs always like me."

I nodded.

Wrong Man said, "Where'd he go, your dad?"

"I don't know."

"Oh, sure you do." Wrong Man got to his feet to get away from Bill. When Bill wants to lick your face he is very hard to stop and about all you can do is stand up. Wrong Man was short for a grown person and chunky, with clear, light-blue eyes. "It's one thing you don't want to tell me certain things, but don't lie and say you don't know when you do. You don't want to get into lying habits, a nice girl like you."

"Well, I don't know where he went. Not exactly."

"Which way was he going when you saw him last?"

Bill was smelling the tires so he would know where Wrong Man had been to in his car. I said, "That's one of those things, like you said, something that I don't want to tell you."

"You mean it's something you do know but you'd like it better if I didn't know?"

"Uh-huh, something like that." I almost turned to look at the creek but made my neck tight and faced him so stiff and hard that my eyes started to water.

Wrong Man nodded and grinned. "Do you know who I am, Jess?"

"No, sir. Not for sure I don't."

"My name is Dudley, Officer Dudley. Some call me the ABC man. That's because I'm the Alcohol Beverage Control officer. One of my jobs is to look for illegal whiskey and put the folks in jail who make it."

"Oh."

"Your dad's been buying sugar again, Jess."

I just looked at him and didn't say anything. Bill was smelling Officer Dudley's pointy-toed boots now because he had stepped in something that Bill was interested in.

"I say your daddy's been buying sugar again."

"He puts it in his coffee."

"Two hundred pounds of it?" When Officer Dudley smiled it made his eyes shiny. It was a dumb thing for me to say that about his coffee but it was over with now and nothing I could do would change it.

"Where is all the sugar at now, Jess?"

"Ah . . ."

Officer Dudley held up a hand. "No, no, that's probably one of those things you don't want to tell me. Am I right about that?"

"Yes, sir."

He put his hands in his hip pockets and looked at the toes of his boots. Someone had shined them up nice for him or else he had done it himself. "Let me ask you this way, Jess. If he's gone how come his pickup's still here?" He pointed at Dad's old Ford truck. "Did somebody come for him? Can you tell me that?"

I just shook my head no.

He scratched his chin. "I've got me a real bad problem, then, Jess. I was hoping that you could help me, but your daddy must have told you to not tell me things, especially not about where he's gone or the sugar and such as that." He took off his hat and ran his handkerchief around the inside. "Am I right so far?"

"Well . . ."

He held a hand out real quick, his palm toward me. "No, uh-uh, wait a minute. A girl shouldn't be asked to do something her daddy told her not to." He put his cap back on, took it off, then put it back on in the exact same place it had been starting out. "Jess, here's the deal. There are some rough ol' boys laying for your daddy. I'm afraid they could be waiting for him right now so they can . . ." He dropped his head to study his shined boots some more.

"So they can what?"

He looked back up kind of worried. "Well, Jess, I'm afraid they're mad at your daddy and plan to hurt him, maybe beat him up. Maybe do something even worse."

"Why do they want to hurt my dad?"

Officer Dudley worked his hat again. "Well, it seems like they got it in their heads somehow or 'nother that it was your daddy who turned them up. They think it was your daddy who told me where they

10

had their moonshine still and now they been sitting in jail for sixty days and working themselves up to get even."

"Did my dad tell you?"

"No, it was some other fellow."

"Then you tell them that. You can't let them hurt Dad for something he didn't even do. You just go and tell them straight out so they'll know."

"I did, Jess." He took off his hat and put it back on like before. "I told them but they don't believe me, and I can't tell them who it really was because I promised, don't you see? I promised the man who really did tell me that I'd never let anyone know. I gave my word on it."

I said, "Why do they call you Wrong Man, anyway?"

It made him smile and admire his boots some more. "That goes back a few years, Jess. The way it happened was I bought me some illegal moonshine whiskey one time. I needed to buy it for evidence, don't you see? The man didn't know who I was so he sold it to me from under the counter of his store. Little old country store and just as I paid him a feller came in who did know who I was and said, 'Did you sell him some shine?'

"The store owner said, 'Sure did,' and the other guy said, 'Well, you just sold to the Wrong Man.' The name kind of stayed with me, Jess." He jabbed his thumb at me and made a *cluck* noise with his tongue.

"You can call me that if you want to, 'cause you and me, we're real good friends already."

I said, "Which do you like best, Wrong Man or Officer Dudley?"

"I like you calling me Wrong Man."

"Well, good."

3

Wrong Man said he had to search our place to look for whiskey-making supplies. He said he knew he wouldn't find anything, but he looked everywhere just exactly like he expected to. I followed him around while he searched all through the house. When he went out to look in the well house I stayed in the kitchen and made myself some food to eat. I planned to go chasing after dad to warn him just as soon as Wrong Man left. I wished he would hurry.

Bill watched him through the screen door and whimpered with his ears up tight. I looked for Wrong Man from out of the kitchen window. After a time he left the well house and walked to the barn. I thought about Dad, floating down Miller Creek on the raft and not knowing there were bad men waiting for him somewhere. It made a feeling come under where my ribs come to meet. It kept getting worse.

Wrong Man came out of the barn and walked toward the chicken house. I didn't know how to get rid of him. I crumbled up some corn bread into a bowl of milk and ate it with a spoon.

I was eating a second bowl of soaky when Wrong Man strolled back into sight and headed off toward Howard's pen. Howard is our bull and we keep him fenced off by himself. When Dad wants a cow freshened he turns her in with Howard. Bill and I have seen that done twice so far.

Wrong Man stopped at the fence and looked at Howard. Howard stared back at him, which is Howard's way. After a minute Wrong Man walked back toward the house. I finished my soaky and went out the back door to meet him.

"I'd like to look at that shed in the bull's pasture," he said. He pointed over his shoulder with his thumb.

Howard's shed wasn't very big. The left side had a door in it and the right side was just an open slant roof for Howard to get under when it rained. Howard never got under it anyway. Even when it stormed hard Howard would stay right out in it because he's so tough.

I said, "Go ahead."

"Well, how about your bull?"

"That's him right over there." I pointed. "His name is Howard."

"I see where he is, Jess. What I want to know is, is your bull mean?"

"Dad says he isn't. Dad says he's just playful but doesn't know his own strength."

"Well, does your daddy go in there with him?"

"Yes, sir. He hits him first, though."

"Hits him?"

"Uh-huh."

Wrong Man turned and looked over at Howard. Howard looked back, of course. "What's he hit him with, Jess?"

"That hammer." I pointed to the sledgehammer, leaning against the gatepost. "He bangs it down on top of Howard's head and it sort of calms Howard down."

Wrong Man gave a little laugh. "I 'spect it does." He picked up the sledgehammer and held it to see what it weighed. Me and Bill stood and watched Howard. Howard chewed cud and watched us back. I was afraid of Howard and so was Bill.

Wrong Man said, "Nothing in that shed, is there, Jess?"

"I don't think so."

He nodded his head.

I said, "Just some big sacks of sugar."

Wrong Man's eyes got big. He bent his knees and turned toward me in a half crouch.

I said, "And whiskey jugs."

15

Wrong Man started to smile and his face crinkled. He jabbed his thumb at me and made that *cluck* sound again. "You're joking with me now, aren't you? Pulling my leg a little bit?"

"Yes, sir."

He looked at Howard and scratched his chin. "Still, if I'm going to call myself searching the premises I suppose I should look everywhere, shouldn't I?"

"I don't know what you're supposed to do, Wrong Man."

Howard gave a little snort and pawed a kick of dust with his front leg because we'd been standing there long enough now. There was something about it when Howard kicked back dust like that. It always made me and Bill back up a step, even with the fence there. Wrong Man saw it and did the same thing with us. He leaned the sledge back against a fence post and brushed his hands together. "I believe you, Jess. I'm taking you at your word."

"You're scared of Howard, too, aren't you, Wrong Man?"

"Heck, no." He took off his cap and put it back on. "I'm just afraid he'd go to acting up and I might have to do something that would hurt him."

I said, "I see," and looked at Bill. When Bill looked back at me I winked at him.

4

I told Wrong Man that I had to get started on my chores because I thought that would make him go on and leave. Instead, he said, "I'll stay for a while and help you out."

"No, I can do it all by myself. You can go on home." Bill and I wanted to go chase after Dad awful bad.

"Tell me what to do and I'll do it."

"I'm used to doing it alone."

"Well, now you've got me to help you."

"You've probably got your own work to do."

"No. Right now I'm all caught up. What do you want me to do first?"

I didn't know how to tell him that I wanted him to go away. There wasn't a whole lot of daylight left any-

17

way and I sure didn't want to go into Corbin's woods after dark because Bill and I could get lost. I didn't believe the stories about old man Corbin's ghost being in there.

Wrong Man fed the chickens while I milked Grace. Then we cut up some logs with the two-man bucksaw and split and stacked the wood around back of the kitchen door. I tried to do a day's worth of firewood work each day in the summer. Then, when winter comes, I can enjoy it and not worry because there's plenty.

Wrong Man talked the whole time, either telling stories or asking questions. "One time I was laying out for some boys, Jess. I knew they had them a still operating somewheres in Taylor's woods, but I couldn't find their path. They were taking different routes to and from their still, don't you see? Most of the time that's the way I find the stills, just follow the footpath and then there it is."

We picked up the last few pieces of split wood. I gave Bill a stick to carry in his mouth. Wrong Man said, "Where's your daddy's path start?" He looked at me squint-eyed and I shrugged my shoulders and carried my load around the house without even once looking toward the creek.

Wrong Man followed me. "So anyways, what I did was I took my bedroll and some can goods and laid out for them and the second night, sure enough, here they come. They were cutting up and loud talking and I'm waiting, all crouched down when they came past. Four of them, walking along single file in the dark."

We piled the split wood on the stack. Bill let me take his stick so I could put it on the pile too. Wrong Man liked to use his hands while he talked. "So, the last one goes by and I just stand up and fall in behind and walk right along with them bringing up the rear. We go maybe a quarter mile like that, walking along together and they're talking back and forth to one another and I know who they are by now. It's the Wilson brothers and Tommy Joe Phelps and a fellow named Cletus from Summerville.

"So we go on and after while Tommy Joe, he kind of slows down and starts looking around, turning his head this way and that way as we walk. We even split up a few times to go around bushes and climb over fallen trees in the dark and I'm worked into the middle of them by now, don't you see? Two up there ahead of me, two behind and there I am. I'm right there in the middle of them, walking along quiet and not saying anything."

I stopped being in a hurry for Wrong Man to go because it was too close to dark now for me to run after Dad. I wanted to know how his story came out, too, because it was a pretty good one.

"There's a half moon but it's too dark to really see anybody, see their faces and tell who they are, but I can see Tommy Joe looking and turning around and trying to figure it out and counting up to five over and over. We walk on like that another few minutes, nobody talking, and finally Tommy Joe just plain stops and turns around and says, "Cletus, how many of us is there?"

Wrong Man had a deep-bellied chuckle and his blue eyes shined. I laughed with him despite my worries about Dad. Bill thumped his tail.

We put the bucksaw and ax away just as the sun set. Wrong Man said, "Has it always been just you and Leonard out here?"

"No, Bill's here."

"I mean besides Bill."

"And there's lots of people that come to dig for the treasure."

"But it's just you and Leonard who stay here, isn't it?"

"Yes, sir. And Bill."

"You say your daddy be back in a few days?"

"Yes, sir."

"How about you? You be all right all by yourself?"

"Sure, and Bill's here."

"Well, if you want you could come stay with me till your daddy gets back. Me and the missus."

"No, I need to take care of things here."

"Yeah, I guess you do." Mr. Dudley got in his car, backed it up in the yard, then drove off toward the road. He honked his horn and held his hand up through the window.

BILL

Night seems darker when Dad's gone. The rain started and thunder boomed from way off and got closer. I wasn't scared of lightning or thunder and I wasn't scared of being alone either. Mostly, I was scared for Dad out there.

Bill stayed right with me until the thunder crashed nearby. Then he grumbled and got up slowly, like a real old dog, circled his tail down between his back legs, and pulled himself under the bed. I talked to him in a calming way and told him how it was just the angels bowling up in heaven, but I don't think Bill knows what bowling is.

I sang some songs in bed and tried to read a frog story by Mark Twain. Most of the time when I read a good story I forget about everything else. But this time I kept thinking about Dad, and how he looked floating away.

Thunder shook the house and Bill cried a little bit. He knows it doesn't do any good to cry but he can't help himself. I got out of bed and looked out the window. Raindrops smacked against it from the outside. When the lightning came I could see the tree limbs whipping in the wind.

Dad keeps two pictures of my mother in a drawer that I take out and look at when he's away. She was very pretty. I don't look like her, except brown eyes, and the dark hair. She was curved and soft looking. I'm skinny and straight.

It seems like I remember her but I know I don't really because she died birthing me. I was what is called *breech* and I think that meant I was facing the wrong way to begin with, feet first, and to make it even worse I was all spread legged. That's all I've been able to find out so far. Dad says it wasn't really my fault but it feels like it was my fault when I think about it.

I watched a cow birth a calf last year. It was wonderful to see but scary, too, and made me think about Mom worse than ever and what she must have gone through because of me.

I took out the pictures and looked at them. It felt exactly like my fault.

5

I punched pillows, pulled cover, and rolled over and back all night to look to the window for daytime to start. I finally gave it up and got up and dressed and ate some eggs and turnips. When first light came I was trotting along with Miller Creek on my right. Bill thought it was a new game, being out early for a run like that. He makes a game of just about everything we do, even when I'm trying to be serious.

The morning broke fine and clear with that good deep smell that the rain brought down with it last night. The birds liked it a lot. I don't know if the weather matters to Bill because he is pretty much the same all the time. Except for thunder.

I ran through the woods alongside the creek and wondered if Dad had woke up yet under his sugar tarp. After a few miles I saw where a tree had fallen across the creek. It was a pine more than a foot thick. I guessed it would have taken an hour for Dad to chop through it.

Dad had four hours or so of daylight to start down Miller yesterday when he left and I was going about three or four times as fast as the current could float him. Take away the hour he had spent chopping through the tree and I felt like I would catch him up before long. I finished the biscuit and started running again.

It was easy stepping because it was almost all big trees and not much short growth. Miller did twist and turn a lot, just like Dad told me. I stayed close to the bank because I didn't want to chance it, missing Dad and running all the way to town with Bill. The sun was well up but we were in deep shadow with the tall trees everywhere. The worst part was spiderwebs across my face and in my hair and making me spit all the time.

A half hour later a little jump-over creek flowed into Miller and just beyond that I came up on Dad poling the raft through a slow pool. Bill saw him about the same time and went to barking. It scared Dad and made him jerk around. But when he saw it was me he flashed mad in his face. "What are you doing here, Jess?"

I stood at the edge of the bank trying to get my breath. "Wrong Man came, Dad. Just after you left. He

24

said there were some men looking for you, waiting for you. He said they wanted to hurt you."

"What?"

"Officer Dudley," I said. "The man you call Wrong Man, he was at the house, just after you left yesterday, and he said—"

"Wait a minute." Dad pushed with the pole to come to our side of the creek. I could tell the water ran deep because it took so much pole. He shoved closer and I leapt across. Bill was right behind me. It was easy for Bill because he's a very good jumper.

Dad poled the raft back into midstream where there was some current to help. "Take your time now, Jess. Tell me everything that happened. And talk quiet."

As I told him about Wrong Man, Dad pushed downstream. He was working very hard at it and not going very fast. It's hard to hurry a log raft that's loaded heavy in slow water with just a pole. Bill stood high on top of the tarp that covered the pile of supplies. It was a new experience for him, so he held his mouth way open so his back teeth would show.

Dad said, "You shoulda stayed home, like I told you."

"But those men, I had to tell you about those men so you'd know."

"There ain't no men, Jess. Wrong Man, he probably just made up that story to trick you. That's the way he likes to work."

"You mean it was a lie?"

"Probably. Wrong Man will lie like a preacher when it suits him."

"How about when he said you made illegal whiskey? Was that a lie? Is that what you do when you leave us? Go off to make whiskey like he said, against the law?"

Dad started to answer but he stopped and bit down on his lip instead. He looked pretty mad and went to working hard with the push pole and glancing back at the woods upstream the way Bill and I had come from. There was only one pole, so I couldn't help. Dad was still mad at me, so Bill came down from the pile and sat by my leg to make me feel better.

There were oak trees and sycamores, tall and strong along the creek. Branches swept up and out from each side. We floated along silently under the high leaf roof that even made the air look green, and smell green too.

One time Miss Pritchett at the library gave me a book about the Indian people that used to live around here. They were called Cherokees. It probably looked the same back then when they had it all to themselves and I could see how they wouldn't want to leave it and be marched off to somewhere else.

We passed another feeder creek, a deeper one along the right bank. Dad slowed us with his pole and looked hard up the side creek. "Remember what that looks like," he said.

"You mean up that creek?"

"Yeah, up there's where I go." He pointed with his finger. "Up that creek there with the raft. Just remember where it is."

"Okay."

Miller began running a little faster with the new water from Dad's side creek. He didn't have to pole so hard to keep us moving. I said, "I'm sorry, Dad."

He looked at me but didn't say anything. I hate that look worse than if he'd yell or something.

"You see, I thought there were some men going to beat you up."

Dad nodded but he kept the look. "I'm thinking that Wrong Man might have followed you. That's why I went on past the little side creek, just in case he's around."

"I didn't see anybody following me, Dad."

He still had the look. I said, "Neither did Bill."

"Wrong Man can follow and you won't know it. I got a feeling he's around here somewheres."

Dad's feeling was right. We came around a bend and the creek opened up. Downstream a ways a fallen tree bridged the water like a footlog. Wrong Man and two others sat on the trunk. Their legs dangled toward the water. Bill gave his little "burf" but he wagged his tail at the same time because he saw Wrong Man and he still liked him from before.

Dad stopped poling but the creek took us to them anyway. Wrong Man stood up and walked off the log to the left side bank. "Place here you can pull her up, Leonard," he said.

When we got close enough Dad reached out with the pole and Wrong Man grabbed the end and pulled us to him. Dad had to brace his feet against it and bend his knees.

The other two men swung their legs and watched. The older one had a rifle across his lap. The other was a boy, about my age or a little older. He had something wrong with his mouth. His teeth were wrong and stuck out and that made it hard to close his mouth so he breathed through it and made a *slursh* sound.

Dad stepped onto the bank, bent down, and pulled the raft up on the gravel. Bill and I jumped off. Dad said, "Wasn't right, you doing my little girl thataway."

"Well, I'm sorry about that, Leonard. I can see how's you wouldn't like it but it's my job to catch you whiskey farmers any way I can."

"What'd you do, follow her this morning?"

Wrong Man nodded. "We slept out in your barn last night. Me and Coy and Drury." He pointed to the two on the log.

"Slursh."

Dad said, "What happens now, Shaft?"

Bill perked his ears at the sound of that name, Shaft. He had never heard a name like that before and thought it was strange and unusual.

Wrong Man said, "Tell me where your still is at?"

Dad said, "I ain't studying you, Shaft."

"You tell me where it's at now and I'll ask the judge to go light on you. Tell him you gave yourself up and showed me to it and maybe you'll get off easy, thirty days or something."

I said, "What do you mean, thirty days?"

Wrong Man said, "I'm afraid your daddy's going to have to go to jail, Jess."

I said, "No." It came out of my mouth real loud and the man with the rifle laughed and Wrong Man said, "Shut up, Coy."

Dad said, "Maybe I don't know anything about a still. Maybe I was just taking a boat ride. You ever think of that?"

Wrong Man looked at me. "Is that the truth, Jess? Your dad, you think he was just taking a boat ride?"

"You lied to me, didn't you? You told me I shouldn't lie because I was a nice girl and you went ahead and told me a big awful lie yourself. What's that make you, then?"

The gun man on the log laughed again. Bill growled and showed him his side teeth.

"Where's the still, Jess?"

"I don't even want to talk to you, Officer Dudley."

"I thought you were calling me Wrong Man."

"That's when I thought we were friends."

Dad said, "This is between us, Shaft. You leave Jess out of it."

"Can't leave her out now, Leonard. She's part of it. You made her part of it, leaving her all alone, a wonderful little girl like that. You go sneaking off to make your bush whiskey.''

I said, ''There weren't any men after my dad at all, was there?''

''Well . . .'' He pushed his hat up off his forehead. ''No, not exactly. But there could have been.''

''What a mean thing to do, and after Bill taking to you so nice and all.''

''I didn't do it to be mean to you, Jess. You'll understand someday when you're older that it's just part of my job.''

''I wouldn't have a job like that,'' I said. ''I'm thirteen and that's old enough to understand that well enough right now.'' Bill growled again because of the way my voice sounded and I reached out to pet him on the head. ''You must have had to think a long time to make up an ugly mean lie like that. It was a powerful lie, I give you that. I don't know what else you're like but when it comes to lying you're chief.''

The older man on the log laughed hard at that. Bill growled even deeper and showed his side teeth some more, which isn't like him at all. The man said, ''Watch out for that old cur,'' and raised his rifle.

Officer Dudley said, ''Put the gun down before you shoot your foot, Coy.''

I said, ''Do you know what a terrible thing it is to be at home and all by yourself and wondering if a gang of men might be beating up on your dad and you can't do anything about it? Just lay there and worry with your mind going?"

Officer Dudley shook his head. "I'm sorry, Jess. You're right, I shouldn't a done it. It was a bad thing and I'm truly regretful. But now, let's forget it and be friends."

"That's what you did before, tell me I could call you Wrong Man because we were such friends then go and lie like that. What an awful thing."

"Well, I said I was sorry."

"Saying you're sorry still don't make it right. And saying you're my friend don't make you one, neither, Mr. Dudley."

"I wish you'd call me Wrong Man again anyway. I truly do want to be your friend."

"I don't think I can be friends with somebody who tells me lies."

"I won't lie any more to you."

"That might be a lie right there, what you just said."

"No, that's the truth."

"Besides, it says it in the Bible, 'Don't lie.'"

"Well, not exactly, Jess. What it says is 'Thou shalt not bear false witness.'"

"What that means is don't tell lies, Mister Shaft Dudley."

He rubbed his face with both hands and said, "All I can do is say I'm sorry and ask you to forgive me for it."

Dad said, "You can let us go, Shaft."

"Not until I find your still. How much farther is it, Leonard?"

"There ain't no still for you to find that I know about."

Officer Dudley said, "What you got running, a couple submarines?"

I said, "I do believe it's the worst thing anybody ever did to me, lying like that and scaring me so bad. My heart beat fast all night, and real hard too. I don't think I'll ever be the same from it."

Officer Dudley turned to the men on the log. "You two go scout around downstream a ways. Each take a bank. His still will be close to the water. When you find it fire off a shot and we'll be along."

The two men stood up. The one with the rifle came to our side, the boy who kept his mouth open walked across to the far bank, and they both started away.

Dad said, "Where'd you find those two, Shaft?"

"Wife's cousins."

I said, "Dad's mad at me now and it's your fault from lying to me like that."

"I'm truly sorry, little daughter."

"I'm not your daughter."

Dad said, "How long we have to wait here?"

Officer Dudley stuck his hands in his hip pockets. "They don't find it in a couple hours I guess we'll all give it up for this time."

I said, "And here I thought you were a friend, and so did Bill."

Dad said, "Fuss at him some more, Jess." He stepped back on the raft, sat down, and leaned back against the sugar stacks. He tipped his hat down over his eyes and crossed his arms over his chest. "Let him have it."

Wrong Man sat on the bank and shaved at a piece of wood with a barlow knife. Bill was interested in what he was doing. "You got some family around, Jess?"

"What do you mean?"

"You have somebody, grandparents or uncles or aunts or something like that?"

I shook my head.

"Anybody you can stay with while your daddy's in jail."

I shook my head again.

Dad said, "She don't need nobody but me."

"She ought to be in school, too, Leonard."

"She don't need to be going to no school. She's got her nose stuck in a book half the time as it is. What she don't learn out of books I can teach her."

Officer Dudley gave the stick to Bill but he dropped it. Bill only likes sticks when someone throws them. Officer Dudley leaned against a tree trunk and lowered his cap down over his eyes, like Dad did.

I would have napped, too, if I had some hat and

there wasn't so much to think about. I walked out on the log and watched the water sweep by under me.

Bill sniffed his way out on the log, stepped by me, and crossed to the other side. He walked around in a circle four times before lying down and closing his eyes. He always does that, walk four circles before he lays down. It's never five circles, it's never three either. It's always four, even at home in his regular bed next to mine. Bill doesn't have any special time to sleep. Daylight is as good as dark for him. The same goes for being awake.

I wondered if Dad would have to go to jail and what would happen to me and Bill. Bill sighed in his sleep about some nice dream he was having already. He doesn't worry about the future the way I do and is better off for it.

6

A gunshot boomed from downstream.

Dad raised his head and so did Bill. Officer Dudley smiled from under his hat. "Sounds to me like we got you, Leonard."

Dad leaned his head back against the sugar sacks. "I don't know what you think you've got, Shaft. I'm gonna finish my nap out."

Officer Dudley said, "Come on, we're all going to have a look at that still. You can deny it and say it's not yours if you want to but I'm going to bust it up and put you under arrest."

Dad stood up slowly and stretched himself. "Tell you what, Shaft. I'll go along with you, and you find a still I'll even help you bust it up, but first, how about making a deal?"

"What kind of deal?"

"You don't find anything, a still or anything, I want you to take Jess on home."

"What about you. What are you planning to do?"

"I'm a free man. I'll do what I please, won't I? You're the one told my girl lies and made her forget to mind and leave home when I told her to stay. Now, least you can do is see her back home safe. You owe me that."

Officer Dudley rubbed his chin. "Let's go see what Coy and Drury turned up."

"You go on ahead, Shaft. We'll be along directly."

Dad watched him walk out of sight then said, "Keep them on this side, Jess."

"What do you mean?"

"On the way back home, stay on this side of the creek all the way."

"Why?"

"My still is right over there." Dad tipped his head toward the far bank. "Just a hundred feet or so up that little side branch creek across stream I showed you. If the wind had shifted Shaft would have caught scent of it."

We started walking and Bill was glad to be moving again. It was the best place I had ever been, this old woods. Bill liked it as much as me. The ground was sponge soft and padded with leaves from forever. Everything else was softer, too, the colors, sounds, and light. Even the time seemed to slow down. Bill scratched around and dug holes to stick his nose down into because the earth smelled good to him and satisfied some sort of need he had. The smell of things is very important to Bill.

I said, "Dudley told that fellow to shoot if he found the still."

"Yeah, I know."

Dad had long legs and I had to run some steps then walk some steps. I said, "Well, if the still's back there, how come he shot his gun off?"

"I don't know. I'm wondering that for myself."

We quick-walked some more and after a while caught up with Officer Dudley. He whipped a dead branch in front of his face for cobwebs. I fell in behind him and Dad tromped along behind me. About every fifty steps Officer Dudley would stop and we'd all listen. Then he'd shout, "Drury, Coy," and we'd listen again.

Dad said, "Those two, they might have been shooting at a snake, Shaft. An ol' possum or something."

Officer Dudley didn't say anything but the next time he yelled there was a yell that came back. "Over here, Shaft."

We crossed a small feeder creek and Bill stopped for one of his big drinks. Bill never takes small drinks like I do or Dad. When he takes a drink it's always a belly washer like he doesn't expect to see water again for a long time. Even at home he never just takes a sip or two from his bowl. He either empties it or leaves it alone. There is nothing in between with Bill when it comes to drinking water.

The two men were standing up ahead. Bill burfed at Coy because he had called him a cur back there at the log. Officer Dudley said, ''Where is it?''

Coy said, ''Right over here.''

''Well, let's have us a look.''

We walked one behind the other up a small rise. At the top Officer Dudley stopped. I looked past him and saw a shed that had been hammered together with odd-sized pieces of wooden boards and tin sheets. He yelled, ''Hello in there,'' and Bill backed away from him with his ears down because it was so loud.

We watched the shack and nothing happened. Officer Dudley said, ''You all wait here, I'll have a look.''

7

Dad smiled as he watched Officer Dudley walk away, so I didn't worry either. Bill sat down close by my right side in case I wanted to pet him while we waited. Drury said, "I like your dog."

"So do I."

"Can I pet him too?"

"If he lets you, you can."

Drury knelt down on Bill's other side and we both worked him over with our hands at the same time. Bill thought it was great and made a groan in his throat. Drury laughed about it and I did too.

It didn't take Officer Dudley very long. He walked back toward us and put his hands on his hips. "You could have looked, Coy. Could have looked and seen what it was before you shot your gun off.''

''Well, it might of been a still, Shaft. How was I supposed to know? Some of them ol' boys will shoot, you come around where they're makin'. What's inside there?''

''Just some old cane poles, couple inner tubes, some funny-books. Must be a kid's place, looks like.''

I took a step down toward the shack. Coy started down with me. He said, ''We can still bust it up, can't we, Shaft?''

''No, course not.'' He put his hand against Coy's chest. ''Stay out of there.''

Drury said, ''What kind of comic books?''

''You stay out too.''

I walked on down and found the door. I heard Coy say, ''How come she can go look and we can't?''

'' 'Cause she won't hurt anything or steal.''

''She might, she might steal a comic book.''

''No, she won't.''

''Stick it down inside her shirt.''

Bill came with me and as soon as I pulled the door open I saw the piece of plywood. It was about four foot square and leaned up against the wall. Before I could stop him, Bill went in there and saw it, too, and it was too late.

Bill is probably the bravest dog in the world except for flat things, like a piece of plywood or a big sheet of cardboard. Flat things scare him. He yelped when he saw the plywood and almost fell over himself getting turned and out the door. He zipped past me and scampered up the hill with his rear end hunkered and his ears slicked back tight. When he had run out of sight I could still hear the leaves churning.

I don't know why flat things scare Bill so bad, although I have studied over it. It might be because a flat thing only has two sides that Bill can see, a front side and a back one. I think Bill wonders where the rest went to. Or maybe Bill's afraid that the same thing will happen to him and he'll turn into a flat dog.

It was dark and musty inside the shack. A washtub, turned downside up in the middle of the floor, had a red candle sat on it. The wax had melted and pooled around the bottom of the candlestick to hold it up. The two wooden crates must have been for seats. I didn't see any comic books until I lifted the tub. There they were, about ten of them along with four cans of pork and beans, a box of matches, and a can opener. They must carry their spoons with them from home.

Three cane poles leaned into a corner. Fishing line was wound around the poles and they had cork bobbers attached. Three inner tubes were stacked in the corner.

There was a slingshot hung on a nail. It looked like a good one, made from a hickory crotch with new rubbers and a leather pouch. Dad made one for me when I was eleven and I got so good with it, Dad said

41

he wanted to put me in a contest for money. He called it a flip sometimes.

The secret to good flip shooting is getting your mind set and not trying to aim. You have to see the rock, in your mind, flying right smack into your target. Then you just let her fly and believe in it and the rock goes where you want it to. Once I learned that, I hit things most every time that weren't too far away. I shot big old round river rocks and kept us eating rabbits all winter. Rabbits make good gravy and I'd make sourdough biscuits to put it on.

Then, one day I took a shot at a robin. I didn't mean it and it was such a long way off that I didn't think there was any chance. After that I threw the slingshot away.

I stepped to the doorway and looked back. Some kids must have a lot of fun here, playing and laughing and wrestling and swimming and fishing. Shooting their flips at empty bean cans and reading comic books at night with the candle, and telling scary stories to each other about how the woods were haunted by old man Corbin's ghost.

I wondered about the kids, who they were and how far away did they live. I wondered if their moms and dads knew about them playing here in the woods that were supposed to be dangerous.

I came out and shut the door tight. The men stood just outside, hands in pockets. Dad said, "Well, Shaft, there's your still, so now you take my little girl on home.''

I saw Bill look down at us between trees then turn and slip back into the woods. He would have come back by now if it was just me, but with strangers here it was taking him longer to get his pride back.

Coy said, "I'm getting mighty hungry, Shaft."

Officer Dudley glanced at me and winked. He must have known that I had seen the beans, too, and it was our secret from Coy. I gave Officer Dudley a favorable nod but I was still mad at him for lying to me so.

Dad said, "How 'bout it, Shaft?"

"I don't know." He shook his head and scratched his chin. "I sure do hate it, not catching you. I like the known seizures best of all."

Coy said, "What's that?"

"A known seizure's where I find the still with the operator on the premises. Not to brag or nothing, but I got more known seizures than anyone in the state. Those are the best, especially if there's some rolling stock to confiscate along with it."

Drury said, "What's that?"

"Rolling stock? That's cars or trucks."

Coy said, "You get to keep them?"

"No, course not. County sells them at auction. Not to brag or nothing, but the money from whiskey cars just about paid for the new schoolhouse."

Dad said, "How about it? I'd like to be on my way

and Jess needs to get back and tend to her chores. You've wasted half my day.''

"Well, come on, then. We can be walking while I think it over.''

We started walking back the way we had come. Wrong Man stepped along at my side. He said, ''You want to wait, call your dog first?''

"No, he'll be along.''

"What happened to him, Jess?''

"Nothing. He's just looking around some.''

"Run off like the devil was chasing him.''

"He does that sometimes.''

"Something scare him? He see a snake or something?''

I shook my head.

Coy said, ''You got anything to eat on your boat 'sides sugar?''

Dad said, ''A cheese sandwich is all. Just barely enough for myself.''

Dad always took enough food for lots of days so that meant he told lies too. It was different from Officer Dudley's lie and not as bad. I caught a quick look of Bill trotting through the trees off to the right.

Drury breathed real loud when we climbed hills. We walked another fifteen minutes before I saw Bill again, closer this time and quartering in toward us just like what had happened didn't mean a thing to him. Coy saw him and said, ''There's that damn old cur.'' Bill gave him a hard look.

Officer Dudley said, "Don't talk bad about that dog. I've taken a liking to him." I think he was trying to get back on my good side so I'd call him Wrong Man again.

Dad was leading the way with his long legs. He talked over his shoulder. "You gonna take Jess back like you promised?"

"I didn't promise, Leonard."

"Yeah, you did."

"No, I didn't."

Bill worked his way up beside me and gave the back of my hand a quick dab to apologize for getting scared like that in front of everybody. I bent over and gave him some good solid pats on his flanks. Drury came up on Bill's other side and scratched under Bill's chin. He said, "I really like your dog."

I said, "I think he likes you too."

Officer Dudley said, "That's a fine dog you got there."

I didn't say anything back to him but I smiled at Drury a little.

8

We moved along in single file with Miller on our left. It wasn't much farther up ahead to where we had left the raft. Dad pointed off to the right, sighting down his arm like it was a gun, "It's shorter back to the house if you cut through that way. Save you half hour's walking."

Officer Dudley said, "What are you going to do, Leonard?"

"Taking my raft on downstream is my plans. Not a thing you can do, Shaft. There's no law says a man can't float on his own raft if he wants."

"I'm going to catch you. You keep making stump whiskey and sooner or later I'll catch you up. You ought to quit it, Leonard. You ought to quit making and quit drinking too. If you won't stop for yourself, think about this wonderful girl here." He put his hand on my shoulder and squeezed it. He had strong hands but it was okay. It was the second time he had said I was wonderful.

Dad said, "You mind your own business."

Bill and I turned to Officer Dudley to see what he'd say. He said, "This is my business. This is exactly my business."

Coy said, "I'm about to perish for some food, Shaft."

I was hungry myself and so was Bill. I said, "Which way did you say was the shortest, Dad?"

He pointed again. "That way. You save yourself walking the big bend in the creek. Only about a mile and you'll come out back of the barn."

I started walking. Drury and Coy came with me. Officer Dudley stayed back and talked to Dad, face to face and no smiling. I used a stick to whip the air in front of my face and knock down webs.

After a few minutes Officer Dudley trotted up and walked beside me. He waved his hands, batting at the air around his ears. "I hate a hair fly worse than anything," he said.

"A what?"

"A hair fly. Whatever they're called, I don't know." He took off his hat and swiped over his head with it. I could see the fly, hovering just out of reach. He put his hat back on. "What do they want, anyway?"

"I guess he wants to get in your hair."

"What good would that do?"

"I don't know."

"There he is again." He went to waving and slapping some more.

Coy said, "Hold still, Shaft." He raised up his gun to point at Officer Dudley. "I'll shoot that sucker, he lands on your head." He laughed at that.

"Worse thing in the world's a hair fly."

Drury said, "No, mosquitoes are worse. You know, at night when you're almost asleep and there's one whining around and you can never slap him in the dark."

I said, "When I light the lamp I can never find him."

Drury said, "Yeah, until you douse the light and almost asleep and there he is again."

Officer Dudley said, "Naw, hair flies are still worse. A mosquito, he's just trying to get him something to eat. You can't blame him for that. But now a hair fly just wants in my hair and I'm not going to let him."

Coy said, "Me neither."

I saw the side of the barn through the trees. Bill ran on ahead to see if everything was okay. Officer Dudley said, "How come for God to make a hair fly in the first place you reckon, Jess?"

"I don't know."

"I mean, what do you figure He had in mind?"

Drury said, "Maybe He just made a mistake."

Coy said, "God don't make mistakes. Everything's got a purpose when it comes to God."

Officer Dudley said, "If it was me, I mean if I was God, what I'd do is I'd just say, 'Look, I made a little mistake here,' and then I'd just do away with the hair flies. Start a hair fly disease or something is the way I'd handle it. Something like a hair fly plague."

Coy said, "He knows what you're thinking too."

"Who does?"

"God. He knows just exactly what you're thinking. What I'm thinking, too, and everybody else."

Drury said, "How does He keep track of it all?"

I thought that was a very intelligent question from Drury.

We came to the edge of the woods and walked to our fence line. Drury held the wires apart for me to duck between. Bill was having a little silly running fit about being glad to be home.

Officer Dudley said, "How about fixing us something to eat, Jess?"

Drury said, "That's not right, asking her to feed us when here we are trying to arrest her pa. Let's go to the car and we can stop at a store down the road."

"Jess don't mind feeding us first, do you?"

"I mind a little bit, but I'll do it."

"Good. What you gonna fix us?"

"I don't know." I pointed to the chicken house. "You go get some eggs and I'll see what else there is. Eggs will at least get you started down the road."

Coy said, "You got any side meat?"

9

Bill trotted along with Officer Dudley and Coy to make sure they didn't bother anything. Drury and I walked to the house and I got out a ham and fed the firebox while he carved off some slabs. I said, "Make one slice nothing but fat."

"Why?"

"To give Coy."

Drury grinned at me about that and turned the ham over. I poured flour and milk into a bowl. My back was to him but I felt him watching me and I wished I wasn't so skinny, and wearing old torn overalls.

I said, "Are you some kind of whiskey policeman too?"

"No, I just came along. Shaft asked me to come

along because . . . Well, he thinks you're real nice or something and wanted me to see you."

"Oh." My face was getting warm from mixing the biscuits. I was hungry, too, and it was getting on toward noon.

"Look here," Drury said. He had sliced a hunk off the ham that was nothing but skin and slick white fat. There were pearl-drops of grease on the side.

"Perfect."

He put the plate of ham and fat down on the table near the stove. "You see the way my teeth are?"

"What do you mean?"

"My teeth. Did you notice how they growed funny? All stuck out and crooked."

"No," I said. "I didn't notice that."

"Aw yeah, you did. Can't help but notice unless you're blind, and even then a blind man could hear the way I talk. It's the first thing somebody sees when they look at me. Like when you first saw me in the woods. You noticed it right off, huh?"

I put the big iron skillet on to heat. "Maybe I did notice, Drury. I don't remember for sure, but even if I did it wasn't as bad as all that. After a while I just didn't pay any attention to it at all."

"There's doctors can fix it. Tooth dentists in the city that know how to work inside your mouth and make it better. It costs a lot of money, though, so I'm saving up."

"How much does it cost?"

"A lot more than I've got. It's four hundred dollars just to start and you have to pay them at the beginning. My oldest brother had it done to him, 'cause his mouth was the same as mine."

I dropped the ham slices into the skillet and the *hiss* noise made my hunger come up. "How much have you saved, so far?"

"Not much, really."

"Are you halfway yet?"

"Ugn-uh."

I looked out of the kitchen window. "Here they come with the eggs."

"Fourteen dollars."

10

ill came into the kitchen first, taking little short steps and clicking his nails because he was excited about us having company. Wrong Man held his hat upside down in both hands to hold eggs. I dripped in a spoon of ham grease to the biscuit dough, stirred, then plopped down big gobs on a baking pan.

Officer Dudley said, "Wood stove makes the best biscuits. I told my first wife, Nell. I said, 'Nell, we ought to get a wood stove just for biscuits.'"

I said, "How many wives have you had?"

"Just the one."

"Then why—?"

Drury said, "That's his joke, calling her his first

wife all the time. She acts like it makes her mad when he says it."

I said, "You fellows can wash your hands."

Drury worked the pump for Officer Dudley, then they traded off. I asked, "How you want your eggs, Drury?"

"Any way is fine."

"Tell me how you like them the best."

"Over light is what Mom calls it."

"Me too," Officer Dudley said.

"Sunny side," Coy said. He sat at the table, ready to go.

I said, "Wash your hands."

Coy said, "You're mighty bossy."

I broke an egg into the skillet. The grease spit and popped, so I moved it to the back.

Drury said, "Can I do something to help?"

"Spoons and all are in there." I pointed. "You can draw water for everybody."

Coy said, "You got any coffee?"

"No."

"I bet you do."

He was right, we did have coffee, but I didn't want to fool with making it unless Drury wanted some.

Officer Dudley set four plates by the stove. I checked the biscuits, forked out the best slice of ham, dropped it on a plate, and flipped the egg over. It was going to be just right if I didn't break the yolk right at the last. Drury watched me all the while and it made me feel kind of tight.

I put two biscuits on Drury's plate and slipped the spatula under his egg. It lifted right out and didn't tear up. I let a little grease drip off back into the pan before sliding it onto his plate. "Here you go."

"Thank you, Jess."

"Get you a biscuit, Officer Dudley."

Coy said, "How about me?"

"You haven't washed your hands yet."

"I don't need to."

"Well, I don't need to fix you any ham and eggs. Or biscuits neither."

"You're too feisty."

Officer Dudley said, "Oh, go wash your hands, Coy."

Coy scraped his chair back and stomped to the sink. "Never heard of ham and eggs and no coffee with it."

Drury said, "This is really good, Jess."

"Thank you."

I carried another egg to Drury and fried Officer Dudley's almost as perfect. He bragged on his ham and his eggs and then said, "These cat heads are real fine, too, young lady."

"What?"

"I said these cat heads are just right." He held up a biscuit and grinned. The biscuits were big but not that

big, and I didn't like him calling them cat heads because it didn't sound nice.

I fried Coy's sunny sides and placed them alongside
the slice of fat. He looked down at his plate. "Ain't
much lean on this meat here."

I broke four eggs into a bowl to scramble for me
and Bill. Bill likes his eggs raw the best but the sight of
him lapping them up doesn't sit right with me. Coy
said it again, "Not much lean on this ham."

"You give it to Bill, then, you don't want it."

"You sure you got no coffee?"

Drury said, "Jess said she didn't, now quit asking
her."

"What's a matter with you?"

I halfed my ham and eggs with Bill and sat down
with my plate next to Drury. I had never cooked for
anybody but Dad and Bill before and I wanted to hear
them say more about how good everything was. Dad
always just ate his food down with no talk about it one
way or the other.

Drury tried to eat nice but his mouth worked
against him and he smacked and gulped and I could
almost cry.

Coy said, "That's the back of the Treasure Farm
other side of the creek there."

Drury said, "I heard about that. About there's
some money buried somewhere."

Coy said, "That's just a figment."

Officer Dudley said, "No, it isn't. Old man Corbin

had money all right, and he was just crazy enough to hide it like he said. He'd wander around a lot. Spent a lot of time just walking in those woods we just come out of. Some say his ghost walks it now and at night you can hear him cackle, 'Heh, heh, heh.' "

Bill barked at Officer Dudley for saying, "Heh, heh, heh," like that.

Coy said, "Maybe those boys of his found it and that's why the one shot the other one and ran off."

Officer Dudley wanted to talk but he had his mouth too full and held up his hand and said, "Um, um," until he got it chewed and swallowed down. "I don't think so. Bobby Daniel and them saw him down Nashville. They say they saw him and he didn't look like a fellow with any kind of money. Said he looked pretty down and out."

Drury said, "Bobby Daniel is bad to drink."

"Yeah, but Cori was with him and she tells it the same way."

Drury said, "What's that Corbin said all the time about sitting on a chair and his wedding ring?"

Coy said, "A figment."

Mister Dudley said, "Corbin told everybody to sit on the throne at sunset and look and see his wedding band. He said the treasure is buried right under that wedding band."

"Just a crazy old man," Coy said.

Drury said, "I'd sure like to find it."

I said, "Bill and I would too."

Drury said, "Maybe we could both go look for it together someday."

I wanted to say okay, but I didn't.

Officer Dudley said, "I know how he does it now."

Coy said, "Huh?"

He pointed at me with his fork. "Her daddy. The reason Leonard don't leave a trail is because he does it all on the creek. His traveling. He floats in with his sugar and all on a raft, don't you see? Then he makes his whiskey somewheres along there. He's got plenty of good creek water, doesn't he? Then, he loads his raft back up with the new whiskey and floats her into town and somebody helps him."

Coy said, "Yeah."

Officer Dudley looked at me. "How long's he stay gone, Jess?"

Drury said, "Don't ask her to tell on her own daddy like that."

Officer Dudley said, "About a week? Ten days?"

Drury touched my arm with his fingers. "You don't have to tell him."

"I know."

I had never been touched by a boy like that.

We went back to eating except for Bill. He was already done and came to sit beside me. Drury was chewing and smacking on his ham and Bill raised his ears and cocked his head at the sound of it. He wasn't trying to be mean but I had to keep grabbing his neck and playing with him or he'd have kept staring and tilting his head and Drury would have taken notice.

Coy said, "Know what we could do, Shaft?"

"What's that?"

"We could wait down at that iron bridge, the one on Sandtown Road. If you're right about him floating into town he'd have to come right under the bridge and we'd be there to catch him with all his new whiskey." He was eating the fat meat now and swallowing fast. His chin was shiny and looked slick.

Officer Dudley said, "That'd work if we knew about when he'd be coming, but I don't want to spend all my time there sitting on a bridge day and night. I guess it could be a week or more."

"You pay me a deputy's wage and I'll stay right there till he comes."

Drury was looking at me again. I could feel his eyes and know his head was turned my way. Officer Dudley sopped up egg yolk with a piece of biscuit. "Board wouldn't allow for that much money. I could talk to them about something like twenty dollars a day, but you'd have to stay all day and all night."

"How would I eat?"

"I'd see you got food brought to you."

"How about coffee?"

"Yeah, I'd see you had coffee and you could use my big tent. What you do, you run a line across the creek at night about a foot or so off the water. Tie a little bell to it up by the tent and anybody goes by rings the bell and you wake up. Arrest him right there on the spot and I'll check on you every morning.''

''What if I arrest him and he says no and just keeps on going?''

''He won't do that.''

''If he does, though.''

''Leonard won't do that. You catch him and he'll be peaceable.''

Drury saw that I didn't like hearing them talk about arresting my dad. He said, ''Sure is a good breakfast.''

''Thank you, Drury.''

''You're welcome.''

I said, ''If I was a doctor and someone didn't have a lot of money, I think I would try to fix them anyway.''

''Well, they don't do that way in cities.''

''I don't see why, not if you asked them. Maybe on a Sunday when the doctor was going fishing or on a picnic and it rained real hard. He could do it then, work on your teeth for free since it's raining outside anyway.''

Officer Dudley said, ''You talking about Drury's mouth?''

Drury said, ''Yeah. I was telling Jess that the doctors want to be paid first and she doesn't think so.''

''He's right, Jess.''

''Maybe you haven't found the right doctor.''

Officer Dudley said, ''No, they're all like that. Everybody wants to be paid for doing their job.''

"But being a doctor should be more than just a job you do for money. It should mean something more than that."

Drury shook his head. "You have to have money to pay."

"Well, then I wouldn't worry about it so much because you look okay the way you are."

"No, I don't."

"Yes, you do. To me you do."

Drury said, "Really?" and grinned with his eyebrows up.

Coy said, "Looks like a Rototiller, you ask me, those big old teeth sticking out." He laughed at his own words and Bill growled at him again. Coy said, "You better watch that old cur."

I said, "Wipe your chin," real harsh, and Bill growled again too.

11

I washed dishes, Drury dried, and Wrong Man put them away while he talked about how bad whiskey was. "Ray Irwin and those two ornery boys of his, Jack and Richard, they used to run a little pot still and sell on Sundays. Reason I couldn't find it was 'cause it was right there inside his chicken house and I never thought to look. Well, it seems Ray had an old rooster got to feeding on his sour mash one day and got so drunk he never was the same and got his days and nights turned around backward. After that old Ray had one rooster would holler sunrise and another would holler midnights."

Every now and then Drury would touch our hands together when I passed him a glass or a plate to dry. The way he did was like an accident each time.

"Whiskey is bad for everybody. People and animals both. I know folks will say it don't hurt them and I know there's people who drink and live to be a hundred, but they'd all be better off without. Every drink they take is against them. There's something about men who drink. Seems like they always do their women wrong."

Coy sat on the front porch and smoked a cigarette. Bill watched him from the screen door. He didn't like Coy being there on the porch and every few minutes he'd come over to the sink to look up at me about it with those frowns on his forehead.

Officer Dudley said, "Do you know who Kenneth Kirk is?"

"No."

"Well, your daddy does. Kenneth used to sell your dad's whiskey on Sundays. He lives right back of Friendship Church and on Sundays after meeting he'd sell off his back porch. And him a deacon too."

I was thinking hard about the talk around the kitchen table and wondering if I should run down the creek again and find Dad to warn him about how they'd be waiting for him under the iron bridge this time. I didn't know if talking about it right in front of me was another Wrong Man trick like before or the real thing this time.

Officer Dudley said, "One Sunday morning I went over to Kenneth Kirk's house and I tell him I'm going to search for moonshine and he says go right ahead.

He says look all you want to but don't disturb his wife 'cause she's real sick and in bed with a fever.''

I scrubbed the frying pan and rinsed it in clear water. I reached it toward Drury. "This is the last." When he took it from me he let his hand stay on mine longer than he had to. I didn't let on that I knew what he was doing but I tried to remember exactly how it felt so that later on, after they had gone, and there was just me and Bill, I could remember the feeling back again and take a long time to study on it.

Wrong Man wiped the tabletop with the dishrag. "I look everywhere in Kenneth Kirk's house, even the bedroom with his wife laying there asleep. Try not to make any noise and I don't find anything, so I go ahead and leave.

"Couple weeks later I try again and it's the same story with Sarah Beth sick in bed again and me not finding any whiskey again. But I know he's still selling Sundays.

"Few more weeks go by and I go over to Kenneth's house to search it again and he says Mrs. Kirk is took sick and please be quiet 'cause she needs her rest and I think, *Well, now, this is very peculiar.* So I go in the bedroom and there she lays in the bed and I say, 'Sarah Beth, I know you're awake and I'm fixin' to snatch back the covers.'

"Sarah Beth just lays there but Kenneth says, 'You can't do that, Shaft. She's naked.' I say I'm snatching covers anyway and I pull them back and there lies

Sarah Beth in a cotton dress, with her shoes on and all tucked around her about twenty pint jars of Sunday whiskey.

"And old Kenneth Kirk acts real surprised and says, 'Where'd you get all that whiskey, Sarah Beth?' "

Drury and I laughed at that. Officer Dudley said, "Way I figure is Kenneth Kirk told her to lie still and close her eyes and act asleep and she was going to stick to it no matter what."

I said, "You probably figured right, Wrong Man."

I had forgotten and called him Wrong Man because the story was so good. He smiled and said, "Thank you for the breakfast, Jess. We'll be getting out of your way now." He touched Drury on the shoulder and said, "Come on, Romeo."

Drury said, "What?" at Wrong Man's back as he went out the door. Drury started for the door and turned and looked at me like he was going to say something else. I looked back at him. His mouth really wasn't all that bad. He nodded his head to me, so I nodded back and that was it.

12

Bill barked and followed the car for a little ways, acting like he was chasing them off. It made Bill feel more important. I sat on the porch step and he came back and yawned. I was kind of tired, too, for a day that was only half over. Bill lay down next to me on the step and waited for me to decide what we'd do.

Grace needed milking and the chickens had to be fed. Weeds were about to take over the bush beans. There was washing to get done and it was easy to remember the way it felt when that boy Drury touched me.

Bill put his paw on my leg. "I know, Bill. I just need to sit here another minute." He came closer so I could scratch under his chin. "I wonder why there's so much fuss about whiskey making? Why doesn't Dad quit if it's something he could go to jail for?"

Bill made a little whimper noise. He likes me to talk to him that way and ask him questions even though he doesn't always understand all the words.

I said, "And what do you think about Wrong Man? He seems like a nice man and I think he likes me and you, but then he's trying to take Dad and put him in jail."

Bill sat up to scratch his side with a back leg. "Now I've got to figure out if all that talk about the iron bridge and waiting for Dad was just to make me go running off again so they can follow me again and find Dad's still this time."

I stood up and got Bill's dish and the milk bucket. Grace gets uncomfortable if I put it off too long. She waited in her stall and gave me that big, brown-eyed look. I got tucked in tight to her with my head pushed into her side. The first few pulls went into Bill's dish and he lapped it clean while I half filled the milk bucket.

I put away the stool and took a drink for myself right from the bucket. I like milk warm like that. "Those men liked us, Bill. Except for Coy. I like them too. Even Wrong Man, and after he tricked us so bad. It's nice to be around somebody who likes us, huh, Bill?"

One of our chickens was sick and weak so all the others were picking at it. The chickens we've got are dumb. I shooed them away and threw feed. Even then, a couple of the chickens wanted to come back and pick on the sick one some more, even with feed there for them that the others were eating up first. They do other dumb things too. The rooster is the dumbest one of all but he doesn't think so.

I scattered the rest of the feed, then picked up the sick one. She was poorly and weak and her feathers were matted and dull. I carried her out to the shed, chopped her head off with the hatchet, and buried her in the side yard. Bill watched everything. I said, "Don't be digging her up, Bill. Just leave her be." Bill ducked his head and licked around his mouth.

One thing Wrong Man didn't know was that Dad's still had been real close when they first saw us on the raft. He must have thought that it was a lot farther downstream, at least a lot farther than the shack that Coy had found. I scratched weeds out of the bean patch with the hoe. It's the kind of chore that doesn't really take a lot of thinking so I can do it while I study on other things.

I knew that I could run down and find that still in about an hour, now that I knew where it was and the shortcut. The problem was I didn't know if Wrong Man was around, hiding again so he could follow me like before. It made me feel mad again to remember the way he had tricked me and lied. A person shouldn't do that to another person even if it was part of his work.

I didn't do a good job hoeing weeds because I tried to glance and look while I worked to see if Wrong Man was peeking around some corner. I never did see him and it didn't feel like he was around. Bill didn't see anything either.

The potatoes weren't quite ready to harvest but I dug up a few for my supper anyway and picked a mess of string beans. I put the potatoes in the oven to slow bake and pulled the ends and strings off the beans. String beans taste better to me if I don't cut them up. Besides, when I cook them whole like that I can eat them with my fingers and that seems better too. Nobody else was there to see me eat anyway. I dropped them into a pot to steam and did some rocking and thinking while things cooked. Bill sat next to me so I could pet his head. I liked petting Bill and he liked it, too, so we did a lot of it.

The first garden picking always tastes best of all. I cut the potatoes in half and chopped butter into the white part. I put some butter on the beans, too, and peppered everything down before I got started. Beans and potatoes go together, so do corn and tomatoes, but that will be another six weeks.

After we got done with the dishes Bill and I went out on the porch to think and talk. I had about made up my mind that I better go find Dad again and tell him about Wrong Man and Coy and what they said about waiting for him at the iron bridge with a bell string. If I still thought that way in the morning, we would go on and do it.

It felt nice when that boy's hand touched my hand. I liked it but something about the memory of it scared me. I told Bill about it while I scratched behind his ears, which is probably his favorite place.

13

I fought in bed again, pulling the cover, twisting this way and the other, and sitting up and laying down. Every time I thrashed around it would wake Bill and he'd come over to my bed and see if I was all right and could he do anything for me. I tried to lie quietly so Bill could get his rest and when I fell asleep, I dreamed about Coy waiting at some iron bridge for Dad to come by. He was drinking a lot of coffee and had that gun with him again.

In the morning I unfolded the map and studied it while Bill smelled around outside for a new spot. The first road to cross the river was called Sandtown Road and it was a good inch and a half or more up Route 10 from the house. Fifteen or twenty miles at least.

I drank some milk and ate a potato left over from last night while I read the map. I didn't put any butter on it this time because it was cold. Just pepper.

Bill and I looked around in the barn to see if Wrong Man had slept there again. There was no sign of him so I got the hoe and went to work in the corn. At the end of the row I turned around and started on the next one. Bill was there. He wanted to help but he's not a very good hand when it comes to garden work. I weeded out the row and turned to the next. "We're going to have to go find Dad and tell him about all that talk, Bill. He's got to know about the iron bridge plans."

Bill looked at me with his tongue out. I worked my way to the edge of our corn patch closest to the woods and leaned the hoe against a stalk. "Ready, Bill?"

We ran to the fence, crawled under, and dashed into the woods. It didn't feel like anybody saw us. We started running toward the creek. Bill couldn't understand why we ran so fast but he kept up anyway because he figured I must have had a good reason. I wanted it to be hard for Wrong Man to follow, just in case he had hid out on us again in the barn or somewhere else.

After a couple of minutes we came to a huge stone boulder about the size of our house except taller. It came almost straight up out of the ground and with lots of hollowed-out places and ledges and parts that

72

stuck out. There was a rock shelf near the ground that made a bench seat. The stone looked like a good place to play and climb if Bill and I had the time and not so much to burden our minds. I figured we'd come back here someday and explore around. I called him over and we sat together and got our breathing back. We waited several minutes. No one came, so I told Bill that it would be all right if we just walked the rest of the way.

Bill went on ahead to make sure the way was safe for me. I followed along and counted squirrel nests. Bill liked the woods as much as I did and when he came to a new place he would stop and wait for me so we could look at it together. Then Bill would find a tree and hike his leg to mark the spot in case he wanted to find it again later on.

We came to the creek and walked up to where we had left the raft yesterday. There was no sign of it, no sign of Dad either. I got real quiet and listened but I couldn't hear anything and neither could Bill.

I crossed over Miller on the log that Coy and Drury had sat on. Bill came along and we made our way back upstream toward the side creek. Dad had pointed over this way and said that Wrong Man could have smelled it if the wind had shifted. I sniffed and looked at Bill, who was smelling the base of a pignut tree.

I yelled, "Dad." Everything got real hushed because the birds quit. "Dad, it's me, Jess."

Some more silence. "And Bill's here."

Bill heard him first and perked his ears. He looked over to our right and I looked too. The leaves rustled then Dad appeared. "Jess?"

14

"And you're sure nobody followed you?"

"We were real careful, Dad."

Bill was busy putting his nose to everything in the little one-room shanty. The place smelled something like bread does when it bakes in a stove and the crust gets brown. There were two big barrels with white cloth over the top.

Dad said, "You better be getting on back to the house."

"What are you going to do?"

"I don't know. You did good to come tell me but I'm not sure what to do about it. Right now I want to stay and finish running this batch and start slopping back."

"Do what?"

Dad shook his head. "Never mind all that. Just go on home and don't worry."

Bill stood on his hind legs with his front paws on the barrel and tried to get his nose under the white cloth for a better smell.

"I'll worry all the time now that I know what you're doing, making whiskey and it's against the law and Wrong Man is after you. And that Coy fellow, he's always got that rifle with him and I think he's mean."

"I can handle those fellows. Wrong Man's been after me for five years and I keep giving him the slip." Dad was smiling at some memory he was having.

"Yeah, but if he catches you one time you have to go to jail, don't you?"

"He won't catch me."

Bill got his nose worked under the cloth. Whatever he smelled made him back his head out and sneeze.

"But what if he does?"

Dad smiled again. "Now that I know he's there I'll wait upstream and around the bend from the bridge, then sneak by after dark. Wait a couple hours and float on by real quiet when he's asleep and not expecting it."

"I almost forgot, Dad. Wrong Man thought of that already. He told that Coy fellow to run a string across the creek at night a foot over the water. Said he could tie a little bell to it by the tent so he could hear if you came by."

Dad laughed. "This will be great! Wait till Wrong

Man finds I've snuck right by him and all his traps and bells and strings and everything.'' He slapped the top part of his leg. ''Just wait till he finds I've slipped right on by and gone to town and got back home.'' Dad did a little dance and clapped his hands together. ''Smoke will come out his ears.''

''Is this some kind of game you play with Wrong Man?''

''No, course not.'' He stopped his dance and looked at me, all frowned up now and serious. ''Making liquor is what pays for things. What do you mean, some kind of game?''

''I don't know. It seems to me you're both having a whole lot of fun with all of it, like playing at a game. Hide-and-seek or something like that.''

''Well, you're just a little girl and you don't understand.''

''How old will I have to be before I understand?''

''A whole lot older.''

''I don't know, Dad. I've been wondering why you drink it like you do, the way it does you, and makes you cry and shake and throw up everything.''

''A man's drinking is his own personal affair.''

''You'd be better off to leave it alone.''

''I can handle it.''

''So you're going to try to get by Coy and his string and everything at the bridge, huh?''

''Yeah, I know how to get around that trick.''

Bill came over and nudged my leg with the side of

his face because he thought we should be getting back home to milk Grace and feed the chickens. I said, "Well, I best get home and start on the chores."

"You did good to come and warn me this time."

I walked to one of the barrels and lifted the cloth. There was a thick foam on top. Dad came up and ran his hand through it and felt it between his thumb and fingers. "Be ready to run in two days."

"What?"

"This batch, I'll run it in about two days then slop back the bit one more time."

"Do you drink this stuff?"

"Lord, no. I make this to sell, not to drink."

"What's that whiskey you drink, then?"

"That's legal whiskey I buy in a store." He pointed to the barrel. "That stuff make you crazy, and blind, and eat out your liver."

"Then why do you make it?"

"Well, to sell."

"But why would you make something to sell that can hurt somebody?"

"Jess, they gonna buy it from somebody anyway and they might as well buy it from me."

"That doesn't seem right, Dad."

"Well, there's not much else for a poor man to do on the kind of land we got, and no wife to help, and no son. I get a dollar a bushel for our corn and that's if I find someone will buy it. Turn that corn into moonshine and it brings twenty, thirty dollars."

"It still doesn't seem right what with all you said about making people blind and their livers and all that."

"We need that money."

"I think I'd rather do without the money than to make somebody blind or sick with their liver."

"Well, you're just too young to know how it is. Just you wait and when you're older you'll understand."

I think that's what Dad says when he's wrong about something and can't think of a good answer. Something was wrong about all this whiskey business. I said, "Come on, Bill. Let's go home and get the work done."

15

A week later Wrong Man drove up into the yard of a morning, raising dust because we needed rain. Bill barked at him, then nosed open the screen door and shouldered on out so that Wrong Man could bend down and pet him in the front yard.

I stayed in the doorway. "Dad's not home."

"I know, Jess." He straightened up, tight faced and not smiling. "I put him in jail last night."

"Oh."

"I'm sorry."

"Why'd you do it, then, if you're sorry about it?"

"I mean I'm sorry about having to tell you, Jess. It's a part of my job that I don't take a liking to." He pulled an envelope from his hip pocket. "Leonard said for me to give this to you and wait here till you read it." He handed it through the door. "I'll stay out here with Bill."

I had never seen Dad's writing before. It was even worse than mine to start with and my eyes were watered up some and it made things look blurry and harder to read.

> *jess   a shelf top of window in well house there a jar say molassis inside some money give to shaft dudley and wen he good and gone go to still and empty two barrels full of sar mash or it will rot and rune barrels a long handle pot dip out then wash in water from crick turn barrels upside down to let dry*

I read it again and it was the same. Bill was fetching a stick for Wrong Man and having a good time. I put the letter in my pocket and opened the door. "You want some coffee or something while you're here? Some sweet milk?"

"Is the coffee made?"

"No, but I can make some. I make it good, Dad says. Good and strong."

"Do you drink it, Jess?"

"Not by myself but when there's someone else I will."

"Well, then, if you'll have some I'll have some along with you."

"Okay."

I ground some coffee beans and filled the thing up with grounds to the mark that said 6. Then I put in four cups of water, sat the pot on the stove, and tossed in some pine kindling. Putting in enough grounds for six cups when there's just water for four is my secret. It comes out strong that way, and dark looking.

I went out on the porch while the water heated. Bill is wonderful to see when he runs, his big fine muscles working in waves, tongue out, and ears flopping. I like it best the way he corners, leaning way to the side and ripping up dirt clods and grass in the air. Wrong Man threw the stick again and Bill started showing out even more now that there were two of us to admire him. When he brought the stick back he took prancy steps like a parade horse with his head held high and fine. He cut his eyes sideways at me to make sure I was getting it all. Bill knows he's good.

Wrong Man took the stick and gave Bill a few pats before he came up on the porch. Bill came right over to me to see what I thought about it and I patted him too. "You ought to be in the fair, Bill."

Wrong Man sat on the porch rail. "You read the letter?"

"Uh-huh. He wants me to send some money to him."

He nodded. "He say anything else?"

"Yes, he did, but it was just for me, so don't be asking about it."

"Okay, okay." He held his hands in the air with his palms out toward me. He had big hands for his size.

I said, "You stay here. I'll be right back."

"Yes, ma'am."

I found the molasses jar where Dad said and counted the money from inside. Wrong Man was still on the bench petting Bill. Bill had stayed with him to make sure he didn't try to follow me and see where the money was hidden. I handed Wrong Man the money. "Would you take this to Dad? There's eighteen dollars."

Wrong Man held the cash money and did his face up funny like something hurt him. "Jess, you sure you want me to?"

"He asked it in his letter."

He moved his lips when he counted. "What he'll do is just get somebody to buy him some whiskey."

"Is he allowed to do that in jail?"

"No, they're not supposed to but they do anyway. They'll always find a way to get whiskey, won't they?"

"I don't know."

"Well, they will. And so what I'm saying is why don't you keep some of this back? You might be needing something for yourself and money spent on whiskey is the biggest waste there is. Be better to just set fire to it, you ask me."

"How long are you going to keep Dad in jail?"

"It's not me that's keeping him, Jess. It's the county, and he's got three more weeks."

"I guess it's his money to do with what he wants."

"Well, now, the way I see it, you do more of the honest work than Leonard so you should have a say in the money." He reached out with two five-dollar bills. "Why don't you keep this here? I'll tell Leonard that it was my idea and I made you keep it. That way if he wants to be mad he can be mad at me and not you."

"I don't need you to be lying to my dad for me. It's bad enough the lies you already told."

He ducked his head down. "I thought maybe you'd forgotten that."

"That won't be for a long time, forgetting that lie. Maybe never. You ought not do things you want people to forget, Wrong Man."

"Well."

"Then you wouldn't have to spend so much time apologizing."

He nodded.

"Something you'd be ashamed of later on, you shouldn't do."

"Okay, Jess. Okay."

"Come on in for some coffee."

It looked good when I poured. It smelled good, too, like it always does, better than it tastes. Wrong Man held his cup in both hands, blew steam, and took a noisy sip with his face wrinkled. "Ahh."

"Don't you want some milk and sugar?"

"No, I like it barefoot."

I stirred some sugar and milk in mine before I tried it. "Still too hot."

"First sip of coffee should cause pain and suffering."

"What for?"

"I don't know, Jess. It's just something I say." He took another sip and smacked his mouth. "Your daddy's right, you do make good coffee."

"Thank you."

"I'll tell Drury, give him something else about you to brag on."

"What do you mean?"

"Drury was real taken with you. He talked about you in the car and wouldn't stop until Coy started teasing him."

"What did he say?"

"Coy?"

"No, Drury."

"You mean what did Drury say to Coy when he started to tease him?"

"No, what did . . . You know what I mean, Wrong Man."

He sipped some more of his coffee but I could see the smile even with the cup to his mouth. "I can't seem to remember now, Jess."

"You go on and tell me now that you've started or I'll tell your first wife how mean you are. What's her name?"

"My first wife?"

"Yes."

"Her name's Nell."

"All right. I'll tell Nell that you've been aggravating me and she won't like it."

"Don't do that." He grinned into his coffee cup again. "Let's see, Ol' Drury started out by carrying on about how pretty you were. 'Don't you think she's pretty,' he'd say. He said you were pretty but you didn't act pretty, if you know what that means."

I didn't know what that meant but it sounded pretty good. I said, "What else?"

"Let's see. He said you were real handy around the house and how clean things were, and how good you did in the kitchen and just went and did the cooking without complaining. That's when Coy got started teasing about how you were too bossy and too bony. He said your backside was too skinny and your ham was too fat. He was just picking on Drury and having fun but Drury didn't like it or think it was funny, him saying anything like that about you. I've never seen Drury have strong feelings before."

I said, "Hmmm," because I couldn't think of anything else. Bill lay down and put his chin on my foot so I'd know right where he was. My coffee had cooled down enough to let me taste of it.

Wrong Man turned up his last swallow and pushed his chair back from the table. I said, "Would you like some more of that?"

"No, that's plenty."

"There's more that I'll just throw out."

"Well . . ."

"It will just go to waste if you don't drink it."

He slid his cup toward me. "Don't like to see anything go to waste."

I filled his cup for him and he said, "Thank you," real polite. I put a little short pour in my cup and put the pot on the cold part of the stove. When I sat down Wrong Man said, "I wish you'd think again about keeping back some dollars."

"I have thought about it. I want to think some more about what you said about me doing most of the honest work. I've been wondering about that very same thing myself lately. But it's best you take all the money to Dad like he asked this time."

"Then there's something else I want you to think about, and don't get mad."

"What's that?"

"Promise first that you won't get mad."

Bill put his chin on my foot again so that I'd know he was still there. "I don't want to promise that. What if I did promise and after that you went and said something that deserves me getting angry about? What would I do then if I'd already promised?"

"What I mean is don't get mad right away. Just think about what I say and hear me out on it first."

"All right."

"Promise?"

"Promise what?"

"Promise that you won't get mad."

"No, it wouldn't be right to promise one way if I might do the other later on. You just go on and say what you have to."

"But I don't want you getting angry with me."

"That's a chance you take sometimes."

Wrong Man opened his mouth to talk, changed his mind, and drank coffee instead. "You make it hard sometimes, you know that?"

"Hard about what?"

"I don't know—everything, I reckon. Here I am a man full grown and wanting to help you out and you're a little ol' girl whose daddy's in jail and it's me that's scared of you."

"Scared?" I had to laugh at that. "You're not scared of me, Shaft Dudley."

"Yes, I am too. I'm scared right now you'll get mad again and talk harsh about a little lie and keep holding it up to me and all."

"Well, I don't know what you expect of a person you tell lies to, Mr. Wrong Man. But if you tell lies to me I'm going to call you down on it every time."

"See, that's what I mean right there." He pointed his finger at me, the one next to his thumb. "What I say is let bygones be bygones, but you don't let nothing slide."

"Well, why do you want me to slide things? Are you fixing to tell some more lies or do something bad and want me to let it slide before I know what it is?"

"No, no." Wrong Man made a lot of different movements with his hands and fingers while he talked. "It's just I wish you'd be a little easier about that sort of thing. You're a mighty young girl to be so set on what's right and what's wrong."

"How much older do I have to be?"

"Well, I don't know there's any certain age."

"Sixteen?"

"No."

"Eighteen, huh?"

"What I mean is maybe you shouldn't always hold people down so tight on it. When you get older you might learn that right and wrong aren't that easy to tell apart all the time and you need a little slack for yourself and some for other folks too."

"How much slack do you want?"

"I want to say some things to you that you might not like to hear at first. I'm going to say them right now, so just . . . what I mean is . . . here it comes and don't be too quick to get mad."

"How quick can I be?"

"Oh, come on, Jess. Back off just a tad, will you?"

"You know what, Wrong Man?"

"What?"

"This is fun, talking like this with you back and forth. I believe this is the most I've ever talked to anybody all in one stretch in my whole life."

Wrong Man just looked at me. He held it for so

long that I started to feel strange about it and wanted him to stop so I said, "What is it?"

"I talked it over with my wife and . . ."

"Which one?"

"Huh?"

"Which wife did you talk it over with?"

"Oh. I talked to my first wife, Nell, and what I want to tell you is that your daddy, when he gets out of jail, he'll go to running shine again and, Jess, I'm going to have to catch him again. Much as I hate to it's my job, and it won't be just twenty-one days this time. It will be sixty days more than likely, because the judge will know about the time before. And then if he gets caught another time it will be six months, or maybe more."

"Well, I'm going to talk to him about quitting the whiskey business."

"He's not going to quit, Jess. I wish he would, too, but it's fast money and he likes breaking the law." He took in a breath, then let it out like he was real tired. "Jess, your daddy's really not much account, and that's the bare truth of it. You deserve something better than you been having. Hard as you work and smart as you are, you should be in school too. Your daddy'd see to it if he wasn't so sorry."

I crossed my arms. "Now I'm starting to think about getting mad at you, Wrong Man, saying that about my dad."

"Don't do that. Please don't. Think about it. If your

daddy keeps on and he goes to jail for a year, where will you be then?"

"I guess I'll be right here. Me and Bill."

"I know. I know you will and I know you do real fine on your own, too, but what I was thinking about and talking over with Nell—my first wife, Nell—is, well, Jess, why don't you come and stay with us?"

"What do you mean, stay with you?"

"I mean come live with us, you and the dog. Just come on and stay with me and Nell and be part of our family. At least try it for a while until your daddy gets out."

"I couldn't do that, even if I wanted to."

"Sure you can."

"No, I couldn't. I've got stock to tend to and the crops to look after. And besides, Bill likes it here."

"We could work all that out, Jess. It would be a pleasure to have you in our house, such a fine young lady. It would save me some worry. It troubles me, you being alone out here."

My lips started kind of squeezing in and letting go and squeezing in. I shook my head no. "Dad needs me. And besides, your wife doesn't even know me."

"Yes, she does. I've told her about you and she'd like to have you stay with us."

I looked back at him and the best I could do was shake my head.

"Well, then, Jess, let me say one more thing."

"What?"

"I want to say please. I want to say please because I've come to care about you, almost like you was my own kin."

I never cuss but I've heard Dad lots of times and I wanted to say, "Dammit," because I knew I was going to cry.

"Durn it, Wrong Man."

16

It makes Bill feel real bad when I cry and he can't do anything about it. He got to crying and whimpering with his chin on my leg and his eyes turned up to me real sad. I could only pat him with one hand so I could keep my face a little bit covered with the other.

Wrong Man put his hand on my shoulder and just let it sit there for a time before he said, "You ain't mad, are you?"

I shook my head.

"Me and Nell never had children of our own, you know, and she loves them. That's why she works volunteer so much at the school and keeps Coy's kids for them and always buys them presents. With me away so much you'd be good company for her. You could help her and she could be a help to you about woman things. And you could show her how to make cat heads."

I had about stopped crying. "Don't call them cat heads."

"Then when your daddy gets out you could come back with him, or stay with us, either one. And then, if I do catch him again, well, then, you'd know you had you a place to come to that was familiar."

"It's nice for you to ask me, Wrong Man, but me and Bill need to stay here and tend the crops and take care of—"

"And the school is there. And a book library and churches."

"I know about the library, and besides, we've got chickens to feed, too, and Grace."

"I'd teach you how to juggle and play the harp, maybe piano lessons with Miss Huxman. She's a widow woman, Mary Lou is. She lives in the old Turner place up on Route Ten. And Nell's a real hand when it comes to sewing. She could make you a dress and show you how."

"Thank you, but I'm staying here and so's Bill."

"There's other young people, and Drury lives down the road."

I shook my head while I sipped coffee. It was too cold now to do any good.

"Well, maybe a visit. Come and spend a day and eat with us. Wouldn't that be nice?"

"Well."

"You could visit your dad first at the jail. Then we'd make ice cream and after while I'd bring you back home."

"Could I bring Bill?"

"Sure. Sure you can. I like Bill as much as you do."

"No, you don't."

17

Wrong Man said he'd come back in the morning, which was Wednesday and visiting day at the jail. "I'll drive you into town and you go visit your daddy awhile then come have supper with me and my first wife, Nell. Not to brag or nothing, but I make the best ice cream there is, and I could ask Drury to come over if you'd like that."

I shrugged my shoulders. "You can if you want to."

Wrong Man pushed his lips out and nodded. "Well, we'll see. You can spend the night if you want or I'll bring you back home before dark, either one."

"Okay."

"Okay, then." He slapped his knees and stood up. "I'll go tell my first wife, Nell, and get my work caught up and be here in the morning about this time."

"Okay, Wrong Man."

"Okay."

Bill barked and ran after Wrong Man's car because it's his nature. Then we got started on the chores together. There was plenty to do before tomorrow and I wanted to go and empty the barrels for Dad so I could tell him it was done and cheer him up a little bit there in jail.

When the sun was high I boiled six eggs for me and Bill and lay down for a nap. I didn't fall asleep all the way but I got close enough to do me some good. Bill rested up some, too, with his chin between his front paws.

We stopped and picked some purple hull peas until all my pockets were full, then crossed the fence into the woods. I ate eggs and peas both while we walked, but Bill just ate an egg after I peeled it for him. He would smell of the peas, but that's all.

The creek was lower than before. When we crossed the foot log I thought about Drury, and seeing him tomorrow, and ice cream too. I wondered what kind of a person Wrong Man's first wife, Nell, would be. I tried out a bunch of different pictures of her in my head. Short and fat, tall and thin, medium? It would be nice if she looked a little bit like my mother and liked me.

It took a lot of trips to dip out enough potfuls so I could get the first barrel down far enough that I could roll it outside and tip it over. The ground corn that had been in there was mushy and soft and Bill ate some from off the ground. I walked down to the creek and back with potfuls of clear water to pour in the barrel. I swished it around and poured it out. The barrel wasn't real clean, but it was close enough and I was tired of it. Anyway, there was another one still to do.

The next barrel took longer and when I washed it out with creek water Bill was eating at the second load of corn mash leavings. I said, "Don't you get foundered, Bill," but he kept right on and acted like he didn't hear. Sometimes Bill won't listen and I have to let him learn it the hard way by himself.

When I got the second barrel back inside and upside down and ready to go back home Bill was gone. I called to him. Then I called again, louder than before, "Bill!"

I walked around the shack. "Bill!" There was a soft grunt from down toward the creek and I fought through the bushes toward the sound. He stood stiff legged with his head down. "Bill?" He didn't move and I dropped to my knees beside him and stroked him easy from his neck on back. His head made little nods but nothing else. "What's wrong, Bill?" I put both arms around his chest. I felt his heart beat strong, but his breath was short and shallow and had the same bad smell Dad had when he had been drinking whiskey for several days.

I guess Bill was the drunkest dog there ever was. It was kind of funny except I know he truly felt bad and probably didn't understand exactly what was happening. I scrambled to his front and held his head in both hands. Bill's eyes looked strange and different and I remembered right then about Dad saying that moonshine could make people blind and got scared for him. "Bill. Bill, look at me, Bill."

And he did. It wasn't much of a look but he raised one eyebrow and looked and I could tell he had sight in there. His tail eased to one side and back, about the slowest wag there ever was. Then he was still again. "Bill, you are bad drunk."

It took a long time with me sitting there holding and petting him and encouraging before he made a move, one step with a front leg. "Atta boy, Bill." After a moment he stepped with a back leg, then another with a front leg. I said, "Where you going, Old Timer?"

He looked at me, then toward the creek, then back at me so I said, "I'll tote you down there," and lifted him up. "But just this once, Bill. If you ever do this again you're on your own."

It wasn't very far down the slope. I gentled him into the water four inches deep and he stood there for two minutes before he lowered his head and took a tongue lap. Just one. I bit my lip to keep from laughing because it would have hurt Bill's feelings.

He felt really bad. I dipped water up with my hands and let it dribble down on the top of poor old Bill's head. He blinked his eyes, which I took to be appreciating on his part, so I did it again. After a few more times Bill took another drink, two tongue laps this time.

"Atta boy, Bill."

Bill tried turning his head next, first to the left a little bit, then to the right. It seemed to tire him. "Don't rush it, Bill. Just take your time."

Then he started whining softly. I don't know what good he thought that would do, whining and crying about how bad he felt, but he kept it up and I said, "Yeah, I know," and things like that. He liked it so I gave him some more of it. "Poor Bill," and, "Poor, poor baby," and some other sympathy talk. He agreed with all of it and felt like he deserved pity because he didn't know this was going to happen.

I dribbled some more cool water onto Bill's head. Dad wanted cool, wet cloths for his head after a drinking spell. I decided that I wasn't going to tend to either one of them if they did this again.

After more of that Bill's stomach started sucking in real hard. I knew what was coming next and climbed out of the creek and sat on the bank. Bill brought up all the corn leavings, every last scrap, it looked like. I hate to throw up and so does Bill but I think it was best for him at the time. He started to act better after that.

Bill turned his back on the stuff floating away from him and took one of his long drinks from the fresh water coming from the other way. He walked out of the creek and shook himself. It was about half as hard as his usual shake so he was still a pretty wet dog when he sat next to me. Bill didn't feel real good, but he was ready to start back home whenever I was. Water dripped from his ears.

18

I walked slow so that it would be easy for Bill and he could keep up. He didn't frisk around or race ahead and back or to the sides either. Mostly he just raised his paws, one at a time, and put them down as easy as he knew how. No stick chasing.

When we got to the big rock I told Bill to lie down and rest while I explored. He didn't make his four circles, he just flopped down and looked up sad. I said, "Poor, poor Bill," for him a few times and patted his head.

The rock had ledges and corners to climb around and over. There were dark, hollowed-out places big enough to hide inside but not big enough to call a cave. I crawled and climbed my way up toward the top. It got high enough to not look down but I did it anyway and was scared just enough to make it even more fun.

I stood on a flat place on the very top and had a long high look around. Bill was laying down there. He was breathing in and out and that was about it.

I was higher than some of the branches. An old oak tree with a big thick trunk had a side limb two feet thick that I could reach up to touch. I wondered if any of those Cherokee people had stood up here where I was. I looked down at Bill again and got swimmy headed, so I eased down to hands and knees.

I started climbing back down and came to another unusual shape in the boulder. My knees were getting sore from scraping the hard, rough rock. I scooped leaves out of a good place to sit and twisted around to get my rear end down first and scooted back. It felt exactly like a chair when I got sat down good, and even had places to put my arms. I settled back nice and straight and took in the scene all in front of me. I sat there a long time because it was a very good place and Bill was getting his rest.

The sun winked through the leaves as it sank lower in the west. It would be sundown before too much longer. The place seemed familiar, like I had been here before, but I knew I never had been. I tried to remember some story I had read with a place like this in it that I might be remembering.

When I climbed down the rock Bill was glad to have me back on the ground where I belonged. The rest had helped him some and we started back toward home. It had felt good sitting up there in that big rock chair and looking out the woods from up high. It stayed on my mind as Bill and I walked along.

After a while I stopped trying to figure it out and all of a sudden everything came together in my head. I stopped between steps and my skin got those bumpy places.

"Bill, that's a throne up there."

Bill turned and cocked his head.

"A throne, Bill, like old man Corbin said. I think that might be it."

Bill just wanted to go home.

"And it will be sundown in a little while too."

I ran back to the rock and started climbing. My heart was going hard and it wasn't from the run or from the rock climb either. When I got to the throne chair and sat back in it Bill was sitting under me with those frowns on his forehead.

A few minutes passed and I could tell about where the sun was going to come out first from behind the limb before it set for good. I waited and tried to breathe regular and just as the bottom of the sun cleared the oak limb I saw old man Corbin's wedding ring hanging down under the branch.

19

"There it is, Bill."

He sat facing up toward me. "The throne, Bill. This is it, buddy. This is that throne that old man Corbin talked about and I'm sitting on it right now. His wedding ring is hanging from that branch right there." I pointed with my finger, but Bill couldn't see it from where he was and just kept looking at me with his tongue hanging out.

"Stay there, Bill. I'm going to see if I can climb out and get the ring. The treasure must be buried down there near to where you are right now. You might even be standing on it. What do you think of that?"

Bill didn't like it when I started working my way out the limb toward the ring. I didn't like it a whole lot myself. I straddled the limb like it was a horse and scooted a few inches while Bill whined and took on.

"I'm okay, Bill," I said.

Bill said, "Oooooh."

If the limb had been laying on the ground somewhere I could have danced and hopped on it and not even thought about falling. I squeezed it between my legs and slid my hands out another three inches toward the ring and Bill said, "Oooooh," again.

"Stop it, Bill. You're making it worse."

I scooted forward two inches and tried to remember what they'd told me that old man Corbin had said exactly. "The treasure is buried under the wedding band." It was a long way to the ground under the wedding band.

"Ooooh." I looked down at Bill and he was taking little nervous up-and-down steps with his front legs, like he was patting the ground.

I reached out, grabbed a branch, and pulled forward another two inches and the branch broke off. Bill barked. "Hush, Bill. I'm all right." I wriggled out a little farther. I could see the wire that circled the limb and held old man Corbin's ring underneath.

It looked like copper wire to me, the ends twisted together and around each other at the top of the limb. I scooted a little more so that the wire was right in front of my face and sighted straight down to the ground. Dead leaves covered everything. I still had the broken tree branch in my right hand and wanted to mark the very place to dig for the treasure later on. "Look out, Bill."

I turned it loose and watched it drop away, hit the ground, and bounce off a couple feet. I would have to remember which way it went from straight down. I tried to untwist the copper. It was strong and thick as a coat-hanger wire. I looked down. "No, Bill. Don't fetch, boy. Put it down." But Bill had it at the balance now and trotted off with it, proud as can be.

"Aw, Bill."

I wondered what else I could drop to mark the spot. A shoe would be good but I didn't want to climb back down the rock without one. Besides, Bill would fetch and carry that too. Then I remembered an egg I had left and reached back to pull it from my pocket. At least there would be some shell pieces left to mark my spot.

Bill had taken the stick off somewhere and left it. He was back under me, looking up. "Now you leave this be, Bill." I reached around the limb and dropped the egg.

Bill was on it in a flash. "Don't eat the shell," I hollered but he had already gulped it down and was looking up for more. I guess his stomach was pretty empty after all that he had put in the creek.

The wire was hard to untwist and hurt my fingers. I needed some pliers, or tougher hands, and I shouldn't have crawled out here in the first place. Now that I was out here I intended to have that ring and drop something straight down to mark the place to dig.

I wondered about Old Man Corbin ten years ago up this same tree, out this very same limb. Which did he do first, bury the treasure or make the tree-climb and hang the ring? And did he really cackle, like they say? I tried cackling myself and as soon as I did the wire gave and started to untwist. Maybe that was the secret, cackling like old man Corbin.

When I got the wire free I turned the loop so I could bring it around and up and there it was, old man Corbin's wedding band, right in front of my eyes. I gripped it tight and ran it off the end of the wire. It slid up and down each of my fingers but fit snug on my left thumb so I let it stay there.

Bill was watching everything. I looked the ground over beneath me, then dropped the wire loop. It bounced away, then back, and Bill was there. He smelled of it real good but let it stay and I started to slide and shinny backward toward the rock.

It was slow and I was careful and even though I was in a hurry I had to stop and look at the wedding band there on my thumb. I said, "Heh, heh, heh," and Bill barked.

20

It was darker down on the ground than it had been up on that tree limb. The woods had a different sense to it now, real quiet and not as friendly now that the sun was down and the birds had quit for the night. I didn't believe in old man Corbin's ghost, though.

Bill didn't like it, either, and wanted to get home. We were both hungry, especially Bill. I found the copper wire and stuck one end down hard into the dirt to mark the place, then we started toward home in the last of the light.

I said, "Tomorrow we'll bring a shovel and come dig real early before Mr. Dudley comes for us."

Bill stayed real close and we walked slowly. "I wonder what we'll find, Bill." I kept talking to take

Bill's mind off of being so scared and worried that Corbin's ghost was following us in the dark. "Ten years, Bill. No telling what's buried down there waiting for us. It could be anything; diamonds maybe, money, or even gold like in a pirate story. Rubies and sapphires. Or, if he was crazy like they say, it could be nothing at all or just a bunch of junk."

There was some light left high in the sky. I could see big things like the tree trunks, but I had to feel out in front to keep from running into bushes and low limbs. I had never worn a ring before either.

"Even if it is junk it will be fun to find it, huh, Bill?"

We guessed our way along as more darkness pushed in, and I caught myself walking with my eyes closed. Something moved in the blackness and rustled the leaves. It sounded loud and heavy but it was probably something that wouldn't hurt anybody. I stopped and squatted down with Bill. "I'm not sure of the way, Bill. It's that way somewhere and everything is okay. I can find it all right, but I'm not sure of the exact best way, so if you know, you just go on and take the lead."

Bill took a different tack from where I had guessed. I followed him, more by sound than anything, and he brought us out right in back of the barn. Good old Bill. He might have been using his nose to smell us back home. We crossed the fence, ate a cold supper, and went to bed. I thought about buried treasure as I lay there, and later on I dreamed about it too.

In the morning Bill was a pest, getting his nose in the way of my shovel as I dug under old man Corbin's ring tree. Bill had always been one to take pleasure from digging in the dirt and now here I was doing it, too, and it pleased him no end. The shovel clanked on something hard and got me all worked up until I dug around and pried it out, a big flat rock.

I backed off and looked up at the ring limb again. It seemed about straight up to me, so I decided to just go deeper. Shovel work is hard. The next time it clanked against something, I knew better than to get excited about it. But I got excited anyway, and it was just another rock.

Wrong Man didn't say exactly when he would come for me, but I wanted to be there. If it wasn't for that I would have rested awhile. Instead, I went to digging harder than before and went, "Heh, heh, heh," the way I imagined old man Corbin must have done.

Bill barked at my cackle noise and the shovel hit something hard again. This time it went *clonk* instead of *clank* and I put my knees on the dirt and went at it with both hands.

"It's something this time, Bill!"

Bill could tell it was something too. He jumped down there with me and sent the dirt flying out behind him. Bill always digs hard like that, fast as he can go. He never digs slowly or medium. A patch of brown metal showed up first, corner-shaped and old-looking. I pushed Bill away and scraped dirt from the top. It was about two feet long, and about eight inches wide with a handle on top. I pulled hard on the handle. Nothing gave way so I pulled again.

"Still stuck, Bill." I used the shovel around the sides, then got down and scooped dirt by hand until I could get my fingers under it and pull up, cackling all the time with Bill barking back at me and both of us grinning at each other and having fun. I heaved again and the dirt turned loose and out came the metal box from old man Corbin.

I had those little tiny raised-up places on my skin, and Bill was smelling the box as fast and hard as he could. It looked like a tool chest, almost like the one Dad kept his truck tools in. It wasn't locked but there was a place for a lock to go if you had one.

"All those people looking for the treasure, Bill, and guess who's the smartest of them all and found it?"

Bill barked twice. I said, "That's right, you and me." I let him smell some more while I rested. "What do you think's in there, Bill?"

Bill had sniffed the box all he needed to. He sat back and licked around his face. Bill doesn't hardly have any lips at all.

"What if it's filled with thousand-dollar bills?"

Bill thumped his tail on the leaves.

I lifted the box out of the hole and sat it next to

Bill. "Pretty heavy," I said. "Too heavy to be paper money. It could be full of rocks, you know. Or horseshoes or something like that. Remember, he was supposed to be crazy."

Bill looked at me and wondered why I didn't just go ahead and open it and see. I said, "Heh, heh, heh," just to tease him some more, and he barked back.

I tried to pry open the top. "It's stuck, Bill." The hinges were rusty and caked with dirt. I used a stick to scrape around in the crack where the lid fit down, cleaning dirt out. "It's been down there a long time, you know." I tried prying the lid again, using the stick this time, and it gave way about an eighth of an inch, showing a thin stripe of clean metal.

"Here it comes, Bill." I worked around the lid some more and it gave some more times. I took a deep breath. "Ready?"

Bill had been ready all along.

I said, "Here goes," and pushed it open.

21

Hundreds of little envelopes filled the box. I had seen them before in a church meeting Dad and I had sat through one time when he forgot and went to town on a Sunday and everything else was closed. People put their money donations in the little envelopes and then dropped them in a pretty basket that got passed about. Dad didn't know that I saw him act like he was putting something in the envelope from his pocket when he really didn't. He gave it a lick and dropped it in just like he was proud of doing his share like the others.

I said, "Old man Corbin robbed the collections, Bill."

Bill smelled them over good. I patted his neck

while I thought it over. "We'll have to find out what church he went to so we can give it back to them."

Bill sneezed.

"Yeah, I know. But it wouldn't be right to keep it. It would be like we were stealing from the church folks."

I picked up one of the small envelopes. I could tell there were coins in there when I gave it a shake. Something was written on the outside with ink. *10, 1916-VF, 16D-EF, 16S-EF.*

Another envelope said, *1, 1901-EF, 02-F, 02-VG, 03-EF.* I opened it and four Indian-head pennies dropped into my palm. The dates were the same as the envelope had said, 1901, 1902, and 1903. They looked like new pennies to be so old. I slid them back inside the envelope and folded it over.

The other envelopes had numbers and letters on them too. It looked like the same person had done the writing each time and I put it all on old man Corbin himself.

And this wasn't church money either.

I put one of the envelopes in my pocket and the others back in the box, then closed the lid. Bill barked twice again and I said, "That's right, pal. Me and you."

We ran all the way home. The box slowed me some because it was heavy, but being excited speeded me up some so it came out about even.

I sat down on the porch step. "We need a place to hide this, Bill."

I thought about the shed in Howard's pasture. He'd be a good guard but I didn't want to hammer him. I thought about burying it but the fresh-dug dirt would show. Then I thought about under the porch where Bill digs anyway. I thought about under the hay pile in the barn.

"I've got an idea, Bill. Come on."

We ran to the barn. Under the workbench was an old metal box that Dad keeps truck tools in and another one for tractor tools. I put Corbin's box in between them and backed off a few steps. It didn't look just right so I put a screwdriver with a broken handle through the place where a lock should go and that helped. Then I turned it halfway to the side and put a greasy rag against it. That was even better and looked like it belonged. I scooped up a handful of floor dust, held it in my palm, and blew it at the box and it looked real good then.

I milked Grace and wondered what Dad would say. We headed for the chicken house. I said, "Wouldn't it be fun if we had someone to tell about all this, Bill? Someone to talk about how much the coins might be worth and what we could buy and things like that."

We threw feed to the chickens and headed for the house. "I wish I was as sure about Wrong Man as you are, Bill. I think he likes us, but I need more time to be sure because every time I start to like him a whole lot he tells a lie or plays a mean trick."

Bill wagged his tail. He can tell about people the

first time he meets them and he's never wrong. I don't know how he does it.

Wrong Man drove up into the yard smiling and waving out the window. I waved back and Bill barked and went looking for a stick in case Wrong Man was ready to throw it. Bill has lots of sticks in different places around our house and remembers exactly where each one is.

Wrong Man stepped out of his car. "Pretty day, Jess."

"Sure is."

"Are you ready to go?"

"I will be. I want to wash up a little bit."

"You take your time." He turned to face Bill, who was coming fast with a stick and grinning. Wrong Man bent at the knees and Bill dropped the stick, then rubbed against Wrong Man's legs and did turnarounds while Wrong Man worked him over with his big hands. Bill thought it was great.

I got out my other pair of overalls because they were newer and cleaner. I had never wanted a dress before. It was just as well that I didn't have one, because I wouldn't have known how to act and hold myself anyway.

I washed my face and neck and watched Bill and Wrong Man out the window. Bill liked him more than anybody else except me. Dad and Bill just barely got along is all.

I gathered up the books I had from Miss Pritchett at

the library. I put the wedding band into the coin envelope and jammed it deep inside my back pocket. They were still playing throw-the-stick-and-bring-it-back. I said, "I'm ready whenever you guys are."

22

"Is this a new car, Wrong Man?"

"No, it's three years old." He pulled out on to the paved road and worked the shifter while he talked. "Belongs to the county but I'm the only one drives it."

Bill had the backseat all to himself and plenty of room but had to stick his face through the window beside my head. The breeze, hard in his face, made him smile and do his eyes half closed and fluttery.

Wrong Man said, "Not to brag or nothing but I'm easy on a car and know how to make one last. I drove a Plymouth ten years and it was still good as new. You could get in that thing and go anywhere you wanted to."

We passed a crossroad and I asked, "Is that Sandtown Road?"

"Yep."

"Is that where the bridge is, the one where you waited for Dad?"

"Yep."

"How did you catch him?"

"We double-belled him."

"What?"

"Double-belled him. I figured you'd go tell him about Coy waiting at the bridge and about stretching a trip line across the water at night. Tie it to a bell." He was waving his hands around as he talked and I wished he'd keep them on the steering wheel, both of them.

"So, what we did was, we tied a line upstream a few feet from the bridge. We figured he'd be expecting that one and be on the lookout. Then, here's the trick part: what we did, we ran another line across just below the bridge where he wouldn't be expecting it. Sure enough your dad found the first one and thought he'd made it but he ran right slap into the second one." He turned to me and smiled. "Ting-a-ling-a-ling."

I said, "Don't you be so happy about it."

"I'm sorry."

"Made a fool out of me again, didn't you?"

"Why, no, Jess. No, I didn't."

"Yes, you did. Just like before with the lie about

some men who were waiting to beat up Dad. That lie of yours that tricked me. This time it was the bridge story and the bell on the string." I turned away from Wrong Man. "See what I mean, Bill?"

"But it was the truth, Jess. Coy waited at the bridge, just like I said. It wasn't a story."

"You knew I'd go tell him, Wrong Man. You used me to turn up my dad again. I don't like it, being so used like that all the time."

"Well, I'm sorry, Jess. I really am."

"You say you're sorry but I don't know if I believe that, either, Wrong Man. You say things you don't mean."

He slowed his driving way down. "I mean it, Jess. In fact, I wish now I wouldn't have done it in the first place."

"You said something else I don't believe."

"What's that?"

"You said you weren't afraid of Howard."

"Well, what I meant there was I wasn't what you call afraid of him. It's more a matter of me having respect for him. That doesn't mean afraid, don't you see? Having respect is different from being afraid."

"I know it's different. What you were was plain scared."

"Just respectful."

"You'd wet your pants if you went in there and Howard gave a snort or something."

"He mess with me, he'd be sorry."

"I think you better take me home."

"Ah, Jess, come on."

"You can't even tell the truth about a little thing like being scared of a bull. Anybody who isn't scared of Howard has something wrong with them. They haven't got good sense."

Wrong Man took in a deep breath and let it out through his lips. "Okay, look here. Suppose I say I was a little scared? If I said it, if I said, 'Yeah, I was scared of Howard.' Well, would you come on into town with me then?"

"Yes."

"All right, then." He pushed in the gas with his foot and we got up some road speed.

I said, "Well, go on and say it."

"Say what?"

"Say you are afraid of Howard."

"I did."

"No, you didn't, Wrong Man."

"Jess, I did so. That's just what I finished saying a minute ago."

"Watch the road!"

He jerked us back to the right side.

I said, "What you said was, you said, suppose you'd admit to it that you were afraid of Howard. Then would I come into town with you? I said, yes, I would. But you haven't said it yet."

"Yes, I did."

I shook my head. "You said, 'What if I said I was

afraid,' or something like that. You still haven't admitted it straight ahead and proper.''

''Okay.'' He bumped the steering wheel with the flat of his hands. ''I admit it.''

''Go on, then, go on and do it.''

''Do what?''

''Admit it good and proper.''

''You're a hard case, Jess.''

''All right, then, if you won't admit it, then stop the car and let me out.''

''Now, Jess, I can't do that. I can't let you out right here on the road. What would you do?''

''I'm fixing to start screaming if you don't.''

Wrong Man took his head way back and closed his eyes. ''Lordy,'' he said. He lowered his head back to straight ahead and pulled the car over on the side and stopped. He half turned toward me in the seat. ''I am afraid of your bull, Jess Gates. Scared to death, as a matter of fact. Frightened and scared and you could even say terrified.''

''Now, wasn't that easy?''

''Well, no, it wasn't. Nothing is easy with you. Can I go on now?''

''Why, sure.''

He got his car back on the road and moving. I turned and looked out the side window so I could enjoy the scenery with Bill and Shaft Dudley couldn't see me smiling so hard.

23

The courthouse is big and all brick except around the windows and doors, where they had used rocks. Wrong Man pulled his car in between some yellow lines where there was a sign on a post that said SHERIFF. He turned the switch key off and looked at his wristwatch. "Right on time." He tapped the watch glass with his fingernail. "Visiting hours start at ten o'clock."

Bill wanted to come with us but I gave him the job of guarding the car and explained how important it was. He laid down on the backseat. Bill likes me to tell him how much I need his help.

Wrong Man led us around to some steps that went down to a side door marked COUNTY JAIL. Inside were some wood benches and chairs all painted the same ugly green. They had been painted over and over. It was probably something they had the prisoners do to keep them busy and out of mischief.

A red-haired policeman in uniform sat behind a steel-barred door. He was watching something through a small window in the side wall. He turned and said, "Morning, Shaft."

"Got a visitor for Leonard Gates."

"I'll bring him around. She can go right on in."

Wrong Man said, "Through that door, Jess." He pointed. "How long you think you'll be?"

"I don't know."

"An hour?"

"Yeah, I guess."

"Okay, I'll meet you here in an hour."

The door led to a room with a halfway-up wall across the center. The top half was some kind of rabbit wire. A lady with straight dark hair was talking to a man through the wire on the far right end. "I'm tired of it," she told him.

The man was tall and big boned with his two upper front teeth missing. He said, "Aw, baby," to her.

She said, "I'm tired of it," again.

On the left side was the little window the red-haired policeman looked through. He wasn't back yet so I pulled the little envelope out of my pocket.

The big man said, "Come on, baby," real quiet this time, but I heard it anyway. I wondered if someone had knocked out his teeth in a fight or if they had just rotted down on their own.

"Just plain tired of it."

I fished out the wedding band and forced it onto my thumb. A door on the other side of the wire opened and Dad walked through. He had on a blue work outfit. When he found me with his eyes they had that off-center look that I knew all about from the times before. He smiled funny, too, and walked up to his side of the wire.

The lady said, "You take all the money and drink, and stay gone all night."

"Aw, baby."

Dad said, "Good morning."

I could smell his whiskey breath through the wire. "Good morning, Dad."

He smiled real silly.

"I found old man Corbin's throne."

"You found what?"

"And you treat me like a dog."

"Aw, baby. I won't do it no more."

"The throne, I found old man Corbin's throne and I sat in it."

"You say that, but then I take what little money we have and bail you out and you're real sweet for a few days, but pretty soon you start in again on the bottle and before you know—"

"Hush, baby. Come on now. I got a job waiting for me. Pay you back in a week."

"You'll be back drinking."

"Aw, baby."

Dad said, "You say you found his throne like they talk about?"

"Yeah, look." I held up my hand with the wedding band on my thumb.

"You ain't kidding, are you? Where'd you find it?" His eyes were more on center now.

"In the woods. And I found the treasure too."

"Keep your voice down." He looked over at the other two. "Come here close and tell me all about it."

24

I told it as quick as I could because it smelled bad with his breath coming straight through the wire at me. After I got through, his eyes were bright and clear. "Old coins like that," he said. "People save those old coins and they're worth a lot of money."

"Look at this." I shook out the 1902 penny. "See how new it looks?"

Dad pressed his face to the wire. "Yeah, it does. That one penny right there, that could be worth a whole dollar by itself, maybe more."

"What you got there, Leonard?" It was the big man from the other end of the room. He stood behind Dad, looking down over his shoulder. "What you whispering over?" I closed my hand on the penny pretty quick.

Dad said, "Get away, Hawkins. Tend your own business, why don't you?"

"What you got in your hand there, little girl?"

"Nothing."

"Show me what you got."

I shook my head at him. He said, "You might as well tell me, sweetheart. Leonard here will tell me anyway. He'll get to needing a drink after and tell me everything I want to know anyway. Won't you, Leonard?"

Dad didn't answer that. The man said, "And besides, I know where you live."

Dad said, "Come on, Hawkins, let us alone."

The man was even uglier when he smiled. He dropped his hand on Dad's shoulder and squeezed. I could tell it hurt from Dad's face, even though he tried not to let it show. The lady watched from the other side of the room and looked sad and sorry about everything that ever happened to her up until now.

The red-haired policeman spoke through a round hole in his window glass. "Everything okay, Gates?"

Dad said yeah, but I said no at the same time.

The policeman said, "Huh?"

Dad said, "Hawkins just wanted to meet my girl. Everything's okay."

I started to say something back but Dad's look made me hold it in. Hawkins smiled at me again. I figured someone had knocked his teeth out in a fight and he probably had it coming too.

The policeman said, ''You go back to your woman, Hawkins.''

''Sure thing, Cap,'' Hawkins said. He smiled at me and it was pretty bad.

Dad leaned closer to the wire again. ''I'm trying to figure out how to sell some of those coins and turn them into cash money without anyone finding out.''

''I don't know how to do that, either, but I can find out.''

''You didn't tell anybody, did you, Jess?''

I shook my head.

''That's smart. Now look here, for right now just don't tell anybody till I have a chance to think it through.''

''I won't.''

''Where did you hide it?''

I said, ''What did that man mean?''

''Who?''

I tilted my head toward the right. ''That big man with his teeth out. What did he mean by saying you'd tell him everything he wanted to know?''

''He was just talking. Where'd you hide the rest of the coins?''

''He said you'd be wanting a drink and tell him everything he wanted to know.''

''Well, he don't know what he's talking about. Did you bury it or what?''

''Is he the one you get whiskey from in jail?''

''Where'd you hide it, Jess?''

130

"He said he knew where we lived too."

"Where'd you hide it?"

I leaned back and crossed my arms. The easiest way would be to tell a lie and say I buried it somewhere.

The lady said, "I get paid tomorrow but I suppose he'd let me have it today if I asked."

"Go ask him now, baby. Go ahead."

"You got to promise, no more drinking."

"I swear," the big man said. "Come on now, I'm your husband, ain't I?" He had his hand raised up.

Dad said, "Tell me where you hid it, Jess."

I looked at Dad and then turned and looked at the big man. He still had his hand up making his bad promise. My thought was he wouldn't keep his promise to the woman.

"Where did you hide it, Jess?"

The lady said, "Okay, I'll go ask him to pay me today."

I thought the lady was being dumb and decided I wouldn't be so dumb myself about Dad anymore. "It's probably best you don't know, Dad."

"What do you mean?" He got his face close again. "Now listen, you're my daughter and you've got to tell me. I'll know how to handle everything from now on."

I shook my head. "I don't know about that, Dad. Maybe I should handle things instead."

"You're just a little girl."

"I found the treasure, though, didn't I?"

Dad stood up and leaned his face tight against the wire so that little squares of skin pushed through. He loud whispered, "Where is it?"

I bit my lip and shook my head again.

"You tell me right now. I'm getting mad."

"I think it's better this way, Dad, where I know and you don't."

"Jess, I'm your father."

"Yeah, I know." I stood up and walked to the door.

Dad hollered, "Jess. Jess, you come back here."

25

"Please tell Officer Dudley that I'll be over at the library."

The policeman said, "Your daddy is hollering after you." He pointed through his spy window.

"I know that. Would you just tell Mr. Shaft Dudley that I'll be at the library?"

"Sure, I'll tell him for you. But you better go see what he wants to say."

"No, I've heard it already."

"How about Hawkins? What did he want?"

"He was . . . I don't know what he wanted."

"He's a bad one, Hawkins."

I let Bill out and we walked around the courthouse yard. He smelled everything and marked a few spots so that other dogs that came through would know that he had been there. I put him back to guard the car some more, picked up my books, and carried them across the street to the library.

Miss Pritchett knows everything about books and she likes me besides. She is old not to be married already but it's not too late if a settled man with some good sense would come along. When she saw me she smiled from behind the big desk and tilted her head to the side like Bill. "Good morning, Jess."

She is full figured, kind of like my mom was except more of it in the chest and hips, and she wears clothes that try to hide it but a person can still tell because it shows anyway. She has dark hair and brown eyes and the best part is her smile.

"Hello, Miss Pritchett."

"Jess, I heard about your father and I'm sorry."

I nodded and sat the books down. She really was sorry about Dad. I can tell just what Miss Pritchett is thinking by how her mouth looks. I said, "Everything is okay and he'll be out before long."

She thought that was sweet and that I was a brave little girl. "Are you staying on the farm by yourself?"

"Uh-huh. Me and Bill."

"And how is Bill?"

"He's just fine." I didn't tell her about how Bill had been sick from getting drunk because I didn't want to explain it and Bill would like it better if we kept it a secret because he was so ashamed of it.

I laid the books on her desk. Miss Pritchett said, "Do you need help with anything, Jess?"

"I might later on but I'd like to try to find some books on my own first."

She nodded and smiled.

There was no one else in the library. I looked under "Coins" and from there went to a word "Numismatics" and learned a number to look for on the shelves and took two books down to carry home.

I went over to the fiction shelves and found the *T*'s. Miss Pritchett was putting the books I had brought back where they belonged. "What author are you reading now, Jess?"

"Mark Twain," I said. "I like him because he is plain speaking and doesn't show off and use all the big words he learned at school."

"I see." Miss Pritchett smiled to herself because she thought that what I had said was cute.

I took down *Tom Sawyer*. Mark Twain's real name is Sam Clemens. I don't know where he got the Mark Twain name from but I thought it was a good one for a storyteller. He must have liked it, too, since he picked it out for himself.

Miss Pritchett put cards in my books that said when I should bring them back. She said, "Are you interested in coin collecting, Jess?"

"Yes, ma'am. Kinda interested, you might say." The coin envelope felt hot in my back pocket and I wanted to tell her about all of it.

"That's nice." She pushed the books toward me.

I said, "Thank you, Miss Pritchett."

"You're quite welcome, Jess." She smiled and I smiled back and started to leave.

"Jess?"

"Yes?"

"Sometime, if I'm out for a drive and pass your place, would it be all right if I stopped by and said hello?"

"Yes, I'd like that. I'd like that a lot and so would Bill."

"Well, I just might do that one day real soon, then."

"Okay." I left the library with my books and wished my dad was nice so that someone like Miss Pritchett would like him and come to live with us. We could be a family.

26

I got Bill and we sat on the grass together under a big elm. We were between Wrong Man's car and the door to the jail so that he would see us for sure, either way. I wished I hadn't promised Wrong Man to go to his house because what I wanted to do now was be at home with Bill and get out all of old man Corbin's coins and spread them out on the bed and look up in the books how much they were worth.

I started reading *Tom Sawyer* and it was good right from the first. The straight-haired woman came out of the jail door looking red-eyed and beat down. If she asked me, I'd tell her to leave that man in jail because she'd be a whole lot better off without the likes of him.

I scratched Bill's neck. Wrong Man thought I was better off without Dad. He hadn't exactly said so, but that's what he meant. He might be right, but it was scary to think about. Being with Dad was all I knew. I touched the coin envelope through my pocket just to make sure it was still there. Bill rolled over on his back so I could get at his chest for a while.

Tom Sawyer was a boy with a lot of devilment in him. He got in fights and went swimming instead of school, and lied to his aunt Polly, who did the best she knew how. Tom was mean to his brother, too, and stole sugar with his fingers.

Tom had to whitewash a big long fence as punishment, but he played a trick on some boys and got them to paint the fence for him by telling them that they couldn't. They give him toys and things just for the pleasure and the privilege. I was reading a part where Tom Sawyer was showing off for some pretty girl when Wrong Man touched my shoulder. I jumped because I hadn't seen him coming and Bill had his eyes closed. Scratching Bill's chest puts him right to sleep.

"You all done seeing your daddy?"

"Yes, sir."

"Ready to go meet Nell, have some dinner?"

"Okay."

We followed Wrong Man to his car. The back of his neck had been shaved up over where his sunburn went. It was warm inside the car and Wrong Man had gotten too much lotion and perfume used on him. Bill sneezed about it and I took down the window on my side.

Wrong Man backed his car onto the street. "Car gets hot when it's all closed up, don't it?"

I said, "Yes, sir," and Bill sneezed two more times.

He glanced down at my books on the seat between us. "What are you reading here, Miss Jess?"

"Things by Mr. Mark Twain," I said. "I started one while I was waiting for you. It's good."

"You got one here about coins." He slid the books around on the car seat. "And here's another one."

"Watch the road."

"You like reading about coins?"

"I don't know. I thought I'd try it and see."

He nodded and looked back down at the books again. "You know who used to mess around with coins all the time?"

"No, who's that?" I knew what he was going to say.

"Old man Corbin. He was a nut about coins. He even got magazines about them, letters, too, and packages brought to him from New York."

I said, "Umm." The coins in my back pocket felt warm again. "In that Tom Sawyer book I was reading when you came, this boy, Tom, was being punished for doing something bad and his aunt made him whitewash a whole big, long fence. And Tom, he tricked some boys into doing it for him awful clever. They even traded him their toys for the honor of doing it."

"How long you been interested in old coins?"

"The boys would first come to tease Tom about having to work while they were going off to swim and fish and play. Tom would just keep on painting and admiring his work and acting like he was having such a good time that pretty soon they'd ask him if he'd let them do a swipe and Tom would say, 'Why, heck no.' He'd say, 'This is too much fun and besides I promised Aunt Polly I wouldn't let nobody pay me so I would let them do some of the whitewash.' So, after a while the boys would offer him things—the rest of an apple or a marble—and Tom would act like he wasn't sure and they'd say please and Tom would—"

"Did you know about old man Corbin being one to read about coins all the time?"

"No."

Wrong Man pointed off to the right. "Back there is where Bob Hill lives. That little white house. Him and Jane."

"Who is he?"

"Bob Hill is the one makes monkey rum."

"What's monkey rum?"

"Monkey rum is the same as regular moonshine except instead of using sugar, like your daddy does, Bob and Jane Hill use molasses and it comes out with a little color in it and kind of sweet."

"Oh."

"Bob Hill has been off to college too."

"Does everyone you know make whiskey?"

Wrong Man smiled and tipped his hat back.

"Seems like it, doesn't it? Either they make it, or drink it, or sell it, or drive it around."

"If everybody does it, why don't you just leave them alone, then?"

"It's not making whiskey that I arrest them for as much as it's not paying taxes on it. Tax evasion, it's called."

"Oh."

He looked down at the books again. "What made you get started on this coin business?"

"What other names do they call it beside moonshine, and monkey rum, and white lightning?"

"Well, let's see. There's corn liquor, and bush whiskey. Some call it skull cracker or pop skull, especially if there's some rub in it. I've heard it called sugar whiskey and stump." Wrong Man was waving one hand around in the air, but at least he kept the other on the wheel and didn't ask me about coins. "Ruckus juice, and radiator whiskey, and tiger sweat. Your daddy calls his blue john. Others are called pine top, and seven stars, and jump steady."

"Jump steady?"

"Uh-huh. And some other names I won't tell you."

"Why not?"

"Some are unfit for a nice young lady to hear."

"Oh."

Wrong Man pointed to a road that branched off to the left. "Up that holler is where I was raised."

I said, "Oh," again. Bill changed sides and stuck his

head out of Wrong Man's window to take the wind on the other side of his face for a while.

"So, you're reading books now about coins, is that right?"

I said, "Why do you call it a holler?"

"What do you mean?"

"You said you were raised up that holler. I wonder where the word *holler* comes from and what it means."

"I don't know. It just means 'holler,' I guess."

"I mean is it supposed to mean 'hollow,' like a hollow place between mountains?"

"I guess it could."

"Or does it mean 'holler' like when someone yells real loud?"

"I don't know, Jess. I never thought about it. I always figured it just meant 'holler' and that was it."

"Or maybe because a holler would carry a long way between those mountains."

Wrong Man turned right onto a gravel road and pointed out his side window. "This is my field over here."

I looked past Bill. The corn was head high. "Your rows sure are laid off nice and straight."

"Thank you." He turned left and drove between some tires that had been painted white and with flowers growing from the inside circle. There were two cars in the yard. One had cement blocks instead of tires.

The house had new paint, white like the tires with the edges and shutters trimmed out in blue. When I got the time I was going to fix up around our place better.

Wrong Man said, "Come on in."

27

We went in the front door and Bill started off to explore and smell. I said, "Come back here, Bill," but he went right on and through a doorway. I called him again but he didn't hear.

Wrong Man said, "He's all right."

I said, "He's never been in anyone else's house before."

"Well, he can't hurt anything."

I had never been in anyone else's home before either. I wanted to be nice and act right, but I didn't know what it was so I just held real still. Wrong Man yelled, "Nell," real loud and a well-turned woman came out into the hall at the far end. She was about as tall as Wrong Man with long, dark-brown hair that had been brushed for a long time. She smiled and wiped her hands on an apron as she came to us.

Wrong Man said, "Nell, this is my friend Jess Gates. And Jess, this here's my first wife, Nell."

"I'm so glad to meet you, Jess." She held out her hand and I took it.

"Yes, ma'am, me too."

She said, "Go wash your head, Shaft."

"What?"

"You smell like a movie star and you let them cut your sideburns too short again."

"It's a new after-shave they got."

"Wash before we eat or it will draw flies in the kitchen."

Wrong Man grinned and touched my arm. "Ain't she something, Jess?"

Bill came back out, clicking his nails on the wood floor. Nell said, "Who is this?"

I said, "That's my first dog, Bill," and Nell laughed. She bent down and Bill went right to her and he liked her a lot. I liked Nell a lot, too, for someone I didn't hardly know. When she smiled she pressed her lips together.

Wrong Man said, "Isn't that Carl Etter's car out front?"

"Yes, he brought some puppies. He said he wants to trade with you. He's waiting around back."

"Trade for what?"

"He said something about a knife."

"I'll go see him about it." He turned and went out the door. I looked at Nell and she looked back while she petted Bill.

"Would you like a glass of iced tea, Jess?"

"Yes, ma'am."

"Well, come and keep me company in the kitchen while I finish up." She half turned and waited for me to walk with her. We started down the hall together and she put her hand on my shoulder.

The kitchen was big. There was real ice from the refrigerator and a glass pitcher of tea with sweat drops on the outside that made me want some.

Bill came with us. Nell poured me a big glass of tea and filled a metal bowl with water and said, "Here you are, Bill," when she put it down on the floor. Bill wasn't thirsty but he took a couple quick licks just to be polite because we were company. I was proud of him.

"Look at those men," Nell said. I looked out the back window with her. Wrong Man and a younger man with short hair were standing, hands on hips, while five puppies smelled around at their feet and tumbled over each other.

I said, "The puppies are cute."

"Yes, they are, but the last thing we need is more dogs. He's got three bird dogs now, and a pack of beagles."

"Does he hunt them a lot?"

"No, hardly ever, Jess. He mostly keeps them

around so he can brag on them. Shaft likes to brag, you know."

I swallowed some tea.

"Do you know how to tell when he's fixing to brag, Jess?"

"No, ma'am."

"He always says, 'Not to brag or nothing,' first. Then he brags."

"Every time?"

"Just about." She watched the men out the window. "Like little children." She sipped her own iced tea dainty and ladylike. "I think they're all that way, don't you?"

I was thinking about what Nell had said and she was right about Wrong Man saying, "Not to brag or nothing," before he started on one. I said, "All what way, Miss Nell?" I took a sip of tea and didn't gulp it this time.

"Please just call me Nell. And let's sit down."

We sat at the kitchen table on wood chairs. Nell said, "I think all men are like that, like little boys that never really grow up all the way. They always need their toys and games while the women take care of things."

"I see."

"Do you know how to tell when he's fixing to tell a lie, Jess?"

I started to say no but stopped and thought about it

and remembered some of the lies he'd told me. I said, "He fools with his hat, doesn't he?"

"Yes, yes." Nell clapped her hands. "He does it every time and thinks he's being so clever. Here we are, us two girls have him all figured out, don't we?"

"We sure do, Nell."

28

Nell and I were working on a second glass of tea and more good talk when Wrong Man and the other fellow clumped up the steps and slammed the screen door into the kitchen.

Wrong Man told Carl to sit down and have some tea. Then he wiggled his fingers at me. "Come with me a minute, Jess."

I followed him into a room with guns and hunting stuff and fishing rods and dead fish and deer necks on the wall. There was a desk and a big glass case with knives on the shelves, maybe a hundred of them, all put down just so. Most were pocket knives and everything was clean and neat.

I said, "Gosh."

Wrong Man nodded and smiled. "Not to brag or

nothing, Jess, but this is probably the best knife collection in the Southeast.''

''Wow.''

Wrong Man put a little wood suitcase on the desk and opened it. There were twelve knives on each side in little grooved-out places so they would stay put and not scrape against one another. He pointed to one with a white handle. ''See this one here?''

''Yeah.''

''That's the one I'm going to trade Carl Etter for.''

''Is it the best one?''

''No, it's the worst, that's why I want to trade it.''

''How about the others?''

He shook his head. ''The others are all good knives. That one is just a cheap drugstore knife. I got four more just like it.''

''You're going to lie to him about it, aren't you, Wrong Man?''

''Why, no, Jess. Not lie, exactly.'' He took off his hat and put it back on. ''I wouldn't do that.'' He closed the case. ''Carl's been lying to me, though, lying about those pups up one side and down the other, and thinks I don't know.''

''So what lie are you going to tell him, then?''

''I'm not. I'm just going to let him believe whatever he wants and let his own greed work against him.''

Bill had his front paws in Carl's lap. He looked at me a little bit ashamed of himself but he didn't offer to get down. Wrong Man opened the case on the kitchen table. "Now, these here are all the knives I've got to sell or trade right now, Carl, except for this one." He pointed at the one he said was cheap at a drugstore, then picked up a black-handled one. "Here's one I think you'll want. It's a genuine Buck knife. Like new, and that's a real stag handle."

Carl handled the knife and squinted his eyes. Then he ran his thumb across the sharp side and said, "Umm."

Wrong Man said, "That'll hold an edge."

Carl wrinkled his face like he didn't think much of that Buck knife at all. He pushed Bill away and leaned forward to look at the others.

Wrong Man looked out the window. "Are you sure Jay Boy sired those pups?"

Carl picked up the white-handled knife. "Yep. If we had papers those pups would bring three, four hundred apiece."

Wrong Man turned around and acted surprised. "Here," he said, "put that down now. You don't want that knife." He took it away and returned it to its slot. "Look at this one here, Carl. It's a Gerber and that's German steel in the blade, real German steel, from Germany."

Carl handled the Gerber and said, "Hmm," again but kept looking at the white-handled pocketknife. I could tell that it was drawing on him. Wrong Man looked out the window and said, "I'll swap you that

Gerber for the little male. I got a feeling that dog will hunt.''

Carl Etter picked up the drugstore knife and smiled. ''Shaft, I sorta like the looks of this here single blade.''

Wrong Man came to the table and sat down. He took off his hat and put it back on. ''I should of known better than to try and fool you, Carl. Look here, take the Gerber and I'll throw in the penknife. It's a North-field. You know I got my heart set on that pup, but come on, you wouldn't take advantage of me that way. I thought we was good friends, you and me.''

Carl Etter smiled. ''We are friends, Shaft, but business is business. We're talking knives here.''

Wrong Man put his elbows on the table and dropped his face down into his palms. ''I shoulda known,'' he said. He shook his head slowly. ''I shoulda known.'' His voice sounded like a sad man about to cry. He kept his head down and swiped through the air with one hand. ''Go on, Carl. Go on, take it.''

Carl stood up. ''I'll leave the pup out back with your beagles, then.''

Wrong Man nodded, his face still in his hands.

''No hard feelings, is there, Shaft?'' Carl held his hand out across the table for shaking but Wrong Man didn't look up. After a moment Carl said, ''Well, I'll be leaving, then.'' He nodded to Nell and me, then looked down at the white-handled knife as he walked to the door, trying hard not to smile.

Wrong Man spoke softly, his face still down toward the tabletop. ''Don't tell it around, Carl. Please, don't be telling it around how bad you beat me on this deal.''

''I won't, Shaft.''

When the screen door slammed Wrong Man looked up with the biggest smile I had seen him make. ''Now, wasn't that pretty?'' he said.

Nell shook her head at him. I said, ''Are you sure you never read that Tom Sawyer book?''

29

Nell had several pots going and I helped while Wrong Man went out to play with his new puppy. There were pinto beans and collards cooking on top of the stove, and sweet potatoes and a turkey in the oven. It all smelled good. I kept the pots stirred and set the table for six people because Drury was coming and Wrong Man's uncle Beeler was coming with his wife, Winnie. Nell said Beeler was turned funny and worked night shift at the sock mill.

I was worried some about the eating that was coming up soon. I wanted to be nice and have manners but I didn't know what all of them were. Except don't eat with your fingers. Except biscuits.

"Look at this, Jess." Nell was looking out the back window and I stood with her and saw Drury had

154

come. We watched Wrong Man show Drury his new puppy. He was talking hard and waving his hands around. Drury picked up the puppy and held it to his chest. He kept glancing at the house because he knew I was in there.

Wrong Man dropped his face down between his palms and shook his head slowly, showing Drury how he had worked it with Carl Etter. Drury smiled and looked at our window again.

I said, "There's a proper way to put down knives and forks and spoons by the plates but I forget how it goes."

"I think the knife and fork go on the right with the spoon on the left," Nell said. "Or it might be the other way around. We don't hold with being real fancy here, Jess. Some restaurant places give you two forks."

"What for?"

"One for your salad, I think. It's shorter than the other."

"Is it okay to eat turkey with your fingers? I do fried chicken that way."

"Sure it is when you're holding a bone, like a wing or drumstick. Now, if Shaft slices off some breast meat for you, it would be better to use your fork."

"I see. Especially if there's gravy on it, huh?"

"I should say so." Nell smiled. "I think a good rule is that it's okay to eat with your fingers if the food has a bone in it."

"Oh." I put down knives, forks, spoons, and said, "How about soup?"

Nell laughed again and I laughed with her.

A car door slammed. Nell looked out the window and said, "There's Beeler."

I watched as the short, white-haired man looked at the puppy. Pretty soon Wrong Man was moving his hands and talking. He put his face down into his palms again, shook his head in a slow manner, then all three of the men had a laugh. Wrong Man even slapped his knees.

Nell said, "Just like children."

I said, "They sure are."

A voice from the hall said, "Nell?"

"In the kitchen, Winnie."

The lady tilted one way then the other as she walked in the door, like a wide duck. She was big around and that made it harder on her. She waved a cardboard funeral fan at her face and wore a cotton dress with little flower pictures on it. "Hello, Nell."

"Have a seat, Winnie, and say hello to Jess Gates. She's my new friend."

Winnie nodded, "Hello there, Jess Gates." She set her eyes on the chair and made a fuss out of getting there, blowing air, tilting back and forth, and fluttering the fan at her cheek. She started to sit down slow, then dropped fast the last few inches and said, "Whew."

Nell brought her a glass of tea and filled my glass

back up before she sat down at the table with us. "It's almost ready. In a few minutes we'll call the men."

Bill came over to meet Winnie and see what she was like. Winnie raised her voice real high and said, "Oh, what a pretty boy, yes him is, him's a pretty boy. Oh, yes."

Bill hates baby talk. He is full grown and much too sensible for that kind of silliness, but he wagged hard and made crying sounds like he enjoyed it just to be polite.

Winnie looked at me while she petted Bill. "Are you the little girl whose father is in jail for bootlegging?"

"Well, yes, ma'am. I'm one of them, anyway. I don't know if there's others."

"Never had a mother, did you?"

"Well, I had one but she died."

"Beeler told me Shaft thinks you're something special. Smart and nice for a girl all by herself out there on that old dirt farm. Says you could amount to something with half a chance."

It was nice to know that Wrong Man had been talking about me in a favorable way. I said, "Did you know that Wrong Man, I mean Officer Dudley, has more known seizures than anyone in the state?"

Nell said, "Not to brag or nothing." She winked at me about it and I winked back to her.

Winnie said, "I don't doubt it. He works at it hard enough, don't he, Nell?"

"Yes, he does."

Winnie pushed Bill away and reached for her tea. Bill wasn't sure if she was through with him so he stayed by her and looked up at her face. She took two big swallows and said, "Show us what tricks your dog does."

"He doesn't do any."

"Well, why don't you teach him some?"

"Like what?"

"Oh, like shake hands or sit up and beg."

"What for?"

"It's just cute and it would show folks how smart he was."

Bill looked over at me. I said, "Bill's smart and he would think that it was silly, shaking hands and begging. He's got too much pride besides."

Winnie made a noise with her mouth that fluttered out some air. "I wouldn't keep a dog didn't do tricks," she said.

Bill came over to lean against my leg. Winnie said, "Why isn't he wearing a collar?"

"He doesn't like them."

"If he was mine he'd like one soon enough."

Nell said, "Go tell the men to come in and eat, will you, Jess?"

30

I had been hoping that Drury would be sitting beside me for supper, but Winnie plopped down on my left and Wrong Man took the head of the table on my right. Drury sat across the table. Wrong Man said the blessing, and it was nice and short because the food looked so good and we had been smelling it all along and waiting.

Drury watched me when he thought I wasn't looking, and when I did look over at him he'd cut his eyes away real fast and act like he had been looking somewhere else the whole time and not at me.

There was a lot of talk around the table and sometimes two at the same time. I didn't want to miss out on any of it, but it was hard to keep up. The food was cooked in a special way and not plain like at home.

There were things added to change the taste a little bit to make it better, and it wasn't just salt and pepper.

Dad was in that jail back there and it didn't seem right, me and Bill having such a grand time. I tried to stop enjoying everything so much. But after a while it made me mad that Dad was keeping me from having fun, so I started having a good time again and Bill did too.

Wrong Man took care of a lot of the talking all by himself. Some of it was his brag and some might have been lies, too, but I couldn't tell because Nell made him take off his hat before he sat down at the table.

Miss Pritchett had sent a book home for me one time that was about good manners and what to say and who opened the door and went in last. A lady had written it and I read it real hard and tried it out at home with me and Dad. But he got tired of it pretty quick and wanted to stop, so I forgot most of it. I watched Nell and acted the way she did because she seemed to be the best one there to go by.

One thing Nell did was keep her left hand down in her lap where nobody could see it, so I did mine the same way except when I used my knife and fork to cut turkey meat into bite pieces. I had a napkin, too, and I'd touch my lips with it now and then just like I'd been doing it for so long that I was used to it.

Nell and I sat up nice and straight instead of slouching down. Wrong Man told it again about how he had traded a bad knife for a good dog. He showed everybody how he had dropped his face down into his hands and Nell grinned at me and winked and looked up at the ceiling like she was praying for some relief.

I looked across at Drury real quick and caught him this time and his face got pink. My face, too, a little bit. When Wrong Man finished his story everybody laughed and smiled like they hadn't heard it before, except Winnie. I laughed, too, but it was mostly at Wrong Man for being so proud of himself all over again.

Bill bumped my leg with his nose and when he did it again I looked down between my knees and there he was with somebody's napkin in his mouth, wanting to play tug with it and take-away. I reached down and took hold of a corner with my lap hand but Bill wouldn't turn it loose. I didn't want anyone to know about it because Bill and I had been doing so good up until now. I pulled a little harder and Bill growled because he thought I was playing too.

Wrong Man was telling a story about what a big fish he caught one time even though he was sick with a fever. I tried to jerk the napkin away from Bill but he was too smart and jerked back and there was a rip sound that made me about half sick. Bill growled again and I covered up his sound by coughing.

Nell said, "Are you all right, Jess?"

"Yes, ma'am."

It was hard to hold on and sit still because Bill kept up those little play tugs. I cut a bite of turkey with my fork and when no one was looking picked it off my plate with my fingers. When I held it down toward Bill he stopped tugging. He held real still and thought about it. It was probably one of the worst problems Bill had ever had to figure out and decide without me to help. I felt sorry for him but I wanted that napkin out of his mouth.

I kept hold of the napkin and moved the turkey meat right up to his nose. That was more than Bill could take and he made his choice right then. I tucked the napkin inside the bib part of my overalls while Bill ate.

Beeler was talking about how the worst thing in the world was Democrats and Winnie watched him with a look that meant, *I wish you would shut up.*

Beeler said, "Roosevelt started it all, way back in the thirties. And that wife of his, that Eleanor."

Wrong Man said, "I thought you liked Democrats." He looked at me and made a real big face-wink and tilted his head at Beeler.

Beeler said, "Ruination of this country."

Winnie blew air out her nose and Bill bumped my leg. I said, "I'd like to know how you got this turkey cooked all the way through and still so juicy and not dried out, Nell."

She said, "I'll write down my recipe for you. The main thing is to cook it real slowly overnight."

I said, "What's that special taste in the gravy?"

"That's sage, Jess."

"Well, it sure is good. It's the best food I ever ate in my whole life."

Nell said thank you, and everybody around the table said it was good, too, but I had been the first.

Bill bumped my leg again. I ate a bite of collards. Bill bumped even harder and growled some more so I looked down. He was looking back up with another napkin and a silly grin.

If we were home I could give Bill a good talking to and make him quit that grinning and understand how it wasn't nice to take folks' napkins from off their laps. There wasn't time now so I cut another piece of turkey meat and traded out with Bill and tucked that napkin under my bib along with the other. They were both a little wet.

Wrong Man said, "Beeler, don't you think that Democrats are better for the workingman?"

"No. They start wars and make inflation go up."

Winnie said, "Democrats do good because they listen to their wives more."

Beeler gave her a look that I would not like to get from him or anybody else.

Bill bumped again and I was pretty sure what it was going to be. There he was with napkin number three and another face grin. I gave him a mean look of my own but it didn't take because Bill knew I really liked him. He bumped again with his nose and I cut turkey.

He took Nell's napkin next and she caught him at it

because she had her hand down there in her lap where it was polite. I didn't remember much of the book about manners but I'm sure it didn't say anything about what to do about when your dog stole napkins at someone else's house. It was one of those things you just had to work on as you went along and do the best you could. Nell looked down, frowned real quick, then she looked at me. I said, "I'm sorry," and she just nodded and closed her eyes for a second and I knew it was all right as far as Nell was concerned.

Bill was bumping again. Winnie said, "Sorry about what?"

I cut a bite of turkey. "Nothing." Everybody was looking at me so I was afraid to swap with Bill and ate the turkey myself. He bumped again and low-growled.

"Why did you say you were sorry?"

I couldn't think of what to say. Wrong Man said, "What kind of corn do you grow, Jess?"

"Yellow dent."

Beeler said, "Best feed corn there is."

Drury said, "They're good roasting ears, too, if you catch them just right when they're in the milk stage."

I slipped Bill some turkey and got the napkin and tucked it away with the rest before I said, "That's true, Drury."

Drury smiled at me. Bill only had one more napkin to go because I was sitting on top of mine to be sure.

Beeler said, "How's your work been, Shaft?"

"Keeps me busy."

"Has it slowed down any from when you first started?"

"Maybe a little. There's probably as many folks making moonshine around here as ever. Not as much transportation as there used to be is all."

"How many arrests you making? One or two a week?"

"One or two a month is more like it. One a week was boom times."

Bill came around to the side between Winnie and me, stretching his neck to look at her lap. I looked, too, and saw that she had her napkin high atop her big belly, which is probably why Bill had saved it for last. He was looking it over hard and making plans.

I caught ahold of his neck and pulled him to me, but he backed out of my hold and was under the table again. It was hard enough to act nice without all this napkin mischief from Bill and I was getting a little bit mad and tired of it.

Bill came around from in back of Winnie on the other side where I couldn't get to him. He had his eyes on her napkin and was thinking about my turkey. I said, "What kind of ceiling is that?"

Winnie looked up with the others and I snatched her napkin and looked back up at the ceiling myself. I had both hands under the table balling it up so I could hide it with the others.

Wrong Man said, "Just regular plaster, same as the walls."

I said, "It sure is pretty."

Bill was worrying at my hands, licking hard and trying to smell between the fingers because there was a napkin in there.

A man came in through the kitchen door and said, "Shaft, can I borry your wheelbarry?"

Wrong Man said, "Help yourself Robert, it's in the shed."

I tucked the napkin in under the bib and the man slammed the door going back out without saying thank you or good-bye or anything else.

Nell said, "Who was that, Shaft?"

"Robert Lord. Works at the mill."

Now I was worried about what would happen when everyone was done eating and looking for their napkins to put down next to their plates.

Nell said, "Everybody save some room for dessert."

Winnie said, "What is it?"

"Apple pie, and Shaft will make ice cream to go with it."

Beeler said, "I'll tell you one thing about the President of this country." He leaned back in his chair and patted his belly with both hands. "He ain't one bit fuller than I am right now."

Bill nosed my leg again. He had gone off and found something else now that I had all the napkins put up. I didn't want to look at the surprise but he bumped again and growled, so I had to before he did worse than that.

It was a little corner piece of waxed paper about two inches on a side. I slipped it away from him because he couldn't hold it tight with his teeth.

Winnie said, "Is that the only trick he does?"

"No, he doesn't do tricks. He's more of a friend."

"I wouldn't keep a dog didn't do tricks."

31

After dinner we all went out on the porch to let our food settle down. Nell said to just let the dishes sit until later. I sat in a two-seat bench that had chains from each end up to the ceiling so a person could swing in it. Drury wanted to sit in it, too, but he wasn't sure so I smiled at him nice to help him out.

When Winnie sat down in a porch rocker she let her dress ride up and didn't notice. With her legs spread out I couldn't help but look up there past her rolled stockings. I was going to be real careful when I started wearing skirts and dresses.

Drury pushed easy with his toes to swing us. He wanted to say something but he couldn't think of anything good. Neither could I, so I helped him push a little bit and looked down at my lap. My mind kept going back to Dad being in jail and the way that Hawkins fellow talked to his wife. I had the feeling that she did all the real work and he just loafed around and drank whiskey. She was hurting herself to stay with him and not doing him any good besides.

I wondered what she would say about me and Dad.

Drury said, "I'm going out for football this year."

"Oh, is that hard?"

"Uh-huh. It's real hard because other boys all try out, too, and some of them are real big."

"I see."

We swang for a while, back and forth. Drury said, "I might get hurt too."

"What?"

"Playing football, I might get hurt."

"Don't do it, then."

Drury said, "Well."

After a while Wrong Man took Beeler and Drury out in the yard to throw horseshoes back and forth at two pipes that he had shoved down in the ground.

Bill went with them and when Beeler threw a horseshoe Bill went chasing off after it. He bit down on it, then let it go, because it didn't feel good to his teeth. If they would have thrown something else he would have been glad to chase and fetch for them.

Nell said, "Beeler looks good, Winnie. He looks a lot better than he did a few months ago."

"He's not good, though. He's stove up in the mornings and won't see the doctor."

Drury threw a shoe that banged into the pipe. He looked over at me on the porch, so I nodded to him that I saw how good he was and it made him smile. Winnie said, "That boy would do better to keep his mouth covered."

Nell said, "He can't help it and he's a real sweet boy."

I said, "He's very nice."

"They're all nice when they're that age, little girl. Men get a few years on them and they start to turn off mean. Beeler's worse all the time." She watched him throw a shoe and sighed out a big breath. "I just pray the Lord takes him soon."

Nell said, "Winnie, now, you don't mean that."

"Yes, I do. I swear, if I had it to do all over again I don't believe I'd marry Beeler."

I said, "Why, won't he do your tricks for you?"

Nell covered her mouth real quick but I could see the smile in her eyes before she looked down at her bosom real quick.

Winnie said, "You're a feisty little thing." She still had her legs apart and I didn't tell her.

Beeler threw another shoe that clanked around the pipe and stayed there. It pleased him so much that he yelled real loud about it and poked Wrong Man in the short ribs. I wanted to try some of that horseshoe throwing myself but I think it was supposed to be horseshoes for the men and sit and talk for the women, so I didn't ask.

Winnie said, "I can see what Shaft likes about you now. It's 'cause you're sassy."

Nell said, "Jess just speaks her mind, Winnie. There's nothing wrong with that."

"It says in the Bible that children should be seen and not heard."

Nell looked at me and shook her head to let me know I shouldn't pay any attention to the things Winnie said.

Drury knew that I was watching him all the time and he didn't know what to do with his hands. Mostly, he shoved them way down in his pants pockets and pulled his shoulders in.

Wrong Man threw a horseshoe and while it was in the air he leaned and waved his hands at it like it was pushing it to the side. Drury laughed at him and glanced at me. I smiled at him nice.

I wondered if Carl Etter had figured it out yet and what he thought of his knife by now. He would know by tomorrow because Wrong Man was sure to go telling it all around and it would get back to him and make him feel foolish and ashamed.

Nell said, "Do you sew, Jess?"

"Just buttons and patches. I know how to darn up a sock hole."

"Sometime come for a visit and you and I will do

some sewing. We could run up a nice dress in an after-noon."

I said, "Okay."

I figured that when Bill and I got home I was going to lay all of old man Corbin's coins out on the bed and look each one of them up in my coin books and find out how much they would bring and write it down. I would talk to Bill about it while I did it and he'd tilt his head.

32

Wrong Man knew a silly rhyme that he'd say while he turned the crank on his ice-cream maker. "You scream, I scream, we all scream, for ice cream." Even after we were all done eating and I said good-bye to everybody and got in Wrong Man's car, the rhyme song kept itself going inside my head. I just couldn't keep it quiet.

"Did you have a good time, Jess?"

"Yes, sir, and that was the best food I've ever eaten."

"What did you like the best?"

"I don't know. All of it."

"The ice cream, I'll bet."

"That was good but so was the rest."

Bill was laying down in the backseat. He was tired,

too, from acting nice and having good manners all day. I let my head lean back against the seat.

"How'd you like the way I traded Carl Etter out of that bird dog?"

"You were clever, Wrong Man. Is he going to be mad when he finds out that you fooled him that way on purpose?"

"He'd have done me the same way, if he knew how."

"How did you know how to work him around that way?"

"Well, not to brag or nothing, but I study people and know a lot about why they do what they do. Most people, Jess, if you tell them they can't have something it makes them want it so bad, they can't stand it. Like Carl and that knife." Wrong Man was waving one hand and driving with the other. "Soon as I told him he couldn't have that knife it started burning on him. He just had to have it then."

I closed my eyes. "Maybe that's the way it is with old man Corbin's treasure. Maybe that's why everybody wants it so bad and looks for it all the time."

"I suspect that's part of it, Jess. He hid it so nobody could ever find it and that makes people want it all the more."

I wanted to tell him right there but kept my own secret.

"Nell likes you a lot, Jess. I knew she would."

"I like her, too, Wrong Man."

"Would you visit again with us? Maybe next week on visiting day. We'll do just like we did today."

"Okay. But you tell Nell that she doesn't have to cook special or anything. Tell her don't go to any trouble about it and to let me help her do chores and just be with her doing her regular things."

"Okay, I'll tell her and that will be just fine."

"And, if she has the time and still wants to, I'd like to try sewing up that dress she talked about."

"I'll tell her that too."

"And tell her I'll wash all the napkins real good and bring them back to her all folded nice."

"What napkins?"

"She'll know."

33

Bill woke up as soon as we pulled into the yard and leaned out the window on my side to see if anything had changed while we were gone. When I opened the door he scrambled out and took off for a run around the yard.

After I got out I closed the door and bent over to look through the side window. "Thanks for the car ride, Wrong Man. Thanks for the nice meal, too, and the ice cream, and for showing me your knives."

"You're welcome, Jess. It was a pleasure for me and Nell both."

Bill was at the side of the house rolling on top of something under his back. He looked funny with all four legs stuck straight up and wiggling around in the air. I said, "Look at Bill."

176

Wrong Man leaned to the window. "Must have found him a dead critter, a dead fish or something."

"Why does he rub on it like that?"

"Dogs, they all do that. I don't know. Some say it's for fleas."

"Why would a dog want more fleas?"

"No, it's supposed to be to keep fleas away."

"Oh."

Wrong Man stuck his hand through the window and said, "See you next Wednesday."

"Okay, Wrong Man." I shook his hand and he drove off with his arm raised up over the top of his car. I waved back and walked over to where Bill was rolling and saw that it was that old chicken with limberneck that I had buried the other day. "Aw, Bill. I told you not to bother her."

Bill kept right on wallering that chicken so I spoke harsh to him. "Come on, stop that and bring her back around to the side of the house."

Bill pretended that he didn't hear. I could have taken the chicken away from him but I didn't want to touch it. "Come on, Bill. You're going to have to put it back right now."

Bill got the chicken in his mouth, dropped it and picked it up, and stuck his rear end up in the air, wanting me to grab for him and chase. "No, Bill. I'm serious now. Come on and we'll put it back. I didn't like it with the napkins either."

I started walking around the side of the house. Bill

ran past me and turned around to drop the chicken on the ground. He backed away a few steps and dared me to try to beat him to it. He would have won because he's faster. I turned the corner and there was the hole in the side yard. Our shovel lay beside it and I knew it wasn't Bill. Somebody must have come and seen the fresh dirt and dug for old man Corbin's treasure while I wasn't home. I didn't like them using our shovel and not putting it back. I didn't like getting mad at Bill for something he didn't do.

"I'm sorry, Bill."

He wagged his tail and pranced around, still wanting me to try for the chicken.

I said, "Drop it," and stomped my foot and put my hands on my hips. Bill still thought I was joking, so I turned my back to him and started walking.

I opened the front door. "Bill, come look at the mess."

34

Whoever it was had tore the place up and turned over chairs and emptied drawers and everything else. All the pots and pans were scattered around the floor along with clothes and blankets. It scared me and made me mad too. Then it made me even more scared. I stood there and looked at the mess and went from scared to mad and back a few times.

Bill was smelling all around the floor to see if he knew who had been here making a mess. Somebody was looking for the coins and the only person who knew about them was Dad and he was locked up back in town. Unless he told.

I started for the door so I could run out to the barn and see if the treasure box was still there but stopped.

Suppose this was someone doing a Wrong Man kind of trick and stirring me up and then hiding out to watch and see where I went. I sure didn't want to fall for that one again.

I hated the way the house looked and the feeling it put inside me. It was like some stranger had slid his hand under my clothes and felt all around.

I looked out the window. Bill was on his back again twisting back and forth on top of that dead chicken. The barn looked the same as always. Maybe they had looked in there already and found old man Corbin's metal box with all the coins. I wouldn't know until I went and looked.

What I needed to do was go straight to a different place just in case there was somebody watching to see where I'd look. I thought some more, then walked on outside. Bill was rubbing his neck on the chicken now, first one side then the other, then back again. I stopped at the gate to Howard's pasture. It would be dark before much longer and Howard never looked this big before. He was watching Bill and trying to figure it out.

"Come here, Bill."

He dropped the chicken and looked up. "Please, Bill. Come over here with me." He came right over and I should have said "please" the first time.

I said, "I'm going in there with Howard."

Bill looked over at Howard and I did too. Howard

180

didn't like it so he raised his head at us to show how big his nose holes were.

"Don't look, Bill. It makes him worse."

The sledgehammer was there but I didn't want to do that because I would be too easy with it and make him madder than ever. "If something happens you'll have to come save me, Bill."

Bill didn't think I should try it, but I had been scared of Howard long enough and figured I could run pretty fast besides. I opened the gate and slipped through it sideways. Bill made a whimper noise and Howard moved a back leg. I swung the gate door shut behind me but didn't latch it.

My line of walk to the shed put Howard off to my left and if I went straight I'd come pretty close to him about halfway. "Now you just behave yourself," I said to him. His eyes were small, black, and hard. "I'm not here to play with you or hit you with a hammer." I kept right on walking like I wasn't scared at all. Howard took a step backward, then another one and tipped his head up to smell of me.

I passed right on, only about four or five long steps away from him. Howard was big. His breath sounded like it came out of a barrel and he had snot running down both sides. "I'm just going in that shed a minute, and I won't bother you."

After I walked by him I didn't turn to look at him over my shoulder but it was hard. When I got to the shed I turned to look. He hadn't moved.

As soon as I shut the door my knees got loose and my body got hot and tired feeling all at once. If there was a chair I'd have sat on it but all there was was a wall to lean against. I was glad that Howard couldn't see me. Bill started barking outside. I thought it was because he was worried about me and wanted to know if I was all right. There was a crack in the wall to peek out of and Howard was still there, looking the other way now. I felt proud that I had faced him down but I still had to go back out there one more time. I hate being scared.

Bill was barking louder about something that had him plenty worked up.

35

There was a gunshot and Bill yelped, then kept right on yelping even harder and I could tell that he was scared and hurt both. I jerked open the door and that Hawkins man was walking at me, holding a pistol with smoke twisting up from the barrel. I hated my father. Bill was on his side, still crying hard for me to do something and if I had a shotgun, I would have done something to Hawkins for sure. Both barrels.

I yelled, "Get away from here."

"Hand over them coins, girl, and I will."

Bill was crying for me even worse. I said, "What coins?"

"You know what coins." He stopped walking and

183

stood about ten feet away. "You hide 'em inside there, did you? Leonard said you hid them somewheres."

Over Hawkins's left shoulder I saw Howard kick some dust back with his front leg and swing his head around. I said, "What did my sorry father tell you?"

Bill was crying and Hawkins smiled. "He told me everything. He told me some of it so's I'd give him a bottle and after he got most of it drunk, he let the rest of it come out too."

Howard was working up a real good mad about Hawkins standing with his back to him that way. He lowered his head and pawed the dirt some more. I said, "Well, if Dad told you, I guess I might as well give it to you, then, huh?"

"Now you're being smart, little lady." He looked to his right and started to turn to look to his left where Howard was getting angered up even worse.

I had to say something real fast. Bill was crying for me. "Look here. Suppose I give you half of it? How about that?"

At first he frowned. Then he smiled. "Why, sure," he said. "Just hand it on over and I'll divvy up with you real fair." He was smiling again and Howard was coming at him now and working up some pretty good ground speed.

I said, "That's real nice of you, mister. Stay right there and I'll see to it you get a nice little extra surprise too."

"Surprise?"

"Uh-huh. Something you don't expect."

Howard dropped his head at the last second and snatched up Hawkins across the back of the knees and tossed him. Hawkins let out a whoop holler as he flipped in the air, arms and legs waving all around. I was running to Bill as fast as I could go before Hawkins came down and before Howard got himself stopped and turned.

Bill's right paw was a red bloody mess and must have hurt him something terrible. As tough and brave as Bill is, he wouldn't carry on like that unless he was scared and the pain was really bad. I picked him up and even with all his suffering Bill gave me a little tongue lick on my neck before he went back to crying and being pitiful.

Howard was turned and coming back for more and Hawkins was crawling and scrambling for the shed door. As he dove through it he pointed the pistol behind him and let fire without taking an aim before he kicked the door shut. Howard stopped and looked at the door like he was making up his mind. He could have knocked it down easy enough if he had the sense to, and I wished he would.

Another shot boomed. Howard jerked back and snorted. Smoke puffed out through a crack in the shed wall. I started running with Bill to the water trough by the barn. There was another shot, but I didn't turn to look. Howard let out a bellow.

Another shot. I bent over and dipped Bill's paw

into the water trough. He cried about that, too, but not very hard because he knew it was for his own good. I swished it back and forth a few times and turned to look back. Howard was standing by the shed like he didn't know what was happening to him or what to do about it. Another shot and a quick shiver went through him. His front leg bent all of a sudden and he took two or three quick short steps to catch himself from falling over.

The shed door swung open. Hawkins stepped out and I didn't have any place to hide. I looked back at him and he didn't smile at all this time. I dashed into the barn. Corbin's treasure box was right where I left it. I snatched it up by the handle, still holding Bill, and took off running.

My first idea was to get into old man Corbin's woods because Hawkins would catch us easy out in the open. I ran between corn rows and heard him yell, "You little witch, come back here."

I had to lay Bill down before I scooted under the fence wire, holding the treasure box. I gathered him back up and struck out for the trees. Behind me Hawkins was running from the barn to the corn field. He was limping and bent to the side, but he was coming at us hard and I wished Howard would have got to him one more time.

It was close to being dark in the woods. When I looked down at Bill he was looking back up at me with sorrowful eyes and I sure did wish I had that shotgun.

Bill couldn't understand why his foot hurt so bad and why I couldn't do something about it.

Bill and the coins put together were a heavy load, but I was running as fast as I could anyway. Before long it would be too dark to see, and then I could stop and think what to do next about Bill's foot and getting away from Hawkins for good. I ran past the rock I had climbed to find Corbin's wedding band. Hawkins shouted something that I couldn't make out. He didn't sound like he was any closer, but he wasn't any farther away, either, so I tried to run faster.

We came to the creek and ran hard alongside it before I almost stumbled and fell because it was too dark to see the ground at my feet now. I slowed down to a walk and tried to listen. My own breathing was loud and so was my heart.

We kept walking, mostly by memory of the time we had followed Wrong Man through these woods. I wished that black-haired woman would have left her man Hawkins stay in jail because that's where he belonged. I was beginning to think that my dad wasn't much better.

36

I was walking, listening hard, and talking easy to Bill when we came to the shack that the kids had made. I knocked softly on the door before I went in and wondered if it was full of snakes laying around in the dark with their tongues going in and out.

Bill whimpered a bit when I laid him and the treasure box down. "I'm right here, pal. I want to light a candle so I can see about you." He cried some more anyway while I walked and felt around until I kicked up against the washtub. It was turned downside up with a candle in the middle like before. I lifted it enough to feel under for the box of matches.

Bill's blood looked black in the candlelight. I didn't know how much of his blood had already come out or how much he had left. I figured that every drop he lost was bad for him. I pulled up my shirt and used my teeth to get a tear started along the bottom and ripped off a long strip about two inches wide.

Hawkins yelled from somewhere outside. It wasn't words, just a loud holler like he'd run into a tree and he sounded plenty mad. I couldn't tell which direction it was, but I figured I better get Bill out of the shack because Hawkins would sure look inside it if he found it. I tied off the shirt bandage and pulled the candle from off the washtub bottom and looked around.

The inner tubes are what gave me the plan. I turned the washtub over right side up and lifted Bill inside it. Then I put in the two cans of beans, the opener, matches, and Corbin's treasure box.

Hawkins yelled again outside somewhere. "I'm gonna get you, you little witch. I got a surprise to give you this time." He was too close to suit Bill and me. I put my arm through the two inner tubes, blew out the candle, lifted up the washtub full of Bill and supplies, then I opened the door.

I couldn't see at all now after the candle was out, but I knew which way the creek was and made our way down there through the trees, feeling the ground with my feet. The bank started falling away steeply so I drug the tub along the ground behind me and half crawled on down into the water. It felt colder in the dark, and wetter too. I was troubled about snake worry again too. Snakes like to stay around water.

Hawkins yelled from somewhere on the other side

of the shack. He called me a witch again and I was getting tired of it. I had some bad names I'd like to call back at him but knew better than to do it and let him know where we were. I put the washtub in the big truck inner tube. It fit inside it just right but Bill was still scared so I had to whisper to him all the time and tell him it was all right and we were going to make it.

I sat down in the other tube and it held me up nice and high. I grabbed on to the washtub handle and kicked against the bank to get us started. When we got toward the middle I could feel the current catch hold of us and push us downstream.

"Here we go, Bill."

I tried to keep all the scared sound out of my voice but he made another pitiful whimper anyway.

"We'll be moving away from that mean fellow and he can't hear us or find us and the water is doing all the work. We can just rest and let the creek take us on away."

I was getting more used to the darkness but there was nothing to see except a star now and then through the leaves overhead. Bill whimpered about his foot and I couldn't get used to that. Every time he made a cry I could feel it draw against my insides.

"Best thing now is to just drift on down until we get to the bridge at Sandtown Road, Bill. Then we'll get out and go up on the road and get someone to give us a ride. I'll get you to a doctor, and he'll help you about your foot." I tried to make it sound easy so Bill wouldn't know how scared I was.

Bill whimpered again but softer this time. If he knew how bad it hurt me he wouldn't have made a sound at all. I said, "It's my fault, Bill, and I'm sorry. I shouldn't have told Dad about the treasure. I should have kept it to myself because if you tell a secret to one person it isn't a secret anymore. Especially somebody like him."

When I stopped talking Bill would begin to cry again so I just kept saying things to him as we floated down Miller Creek in the night. It helped calm me too. I could hear things moving in the bushes and there was something big that splashed through the creek once, but I kept talking anyway and hoped it was a deer.

After a while the bullfrogs started, then a screech owl, and some whippoorwills. Pretty soon the woods were full of sounds to keep us company. Bill quieted down, so I stopped talking and we floated through the darkness. I even got sleepy but stayed awake because Hawkins was still around somewhere, and because of snakes.

A big full moon would have helped, but there wasn't any. The creek began to run a little harder, and I could hear it splash and gurgle downstream. When we came to the riffles I got out of my tube and waded so I could walk Bill through easy and be sure that he didn't spill over.

There was just enough starlight to make little sparkle places in the riffles. The creek was wider, shallower, and faster. A couple times Bill's tub scraped bottom and I had to carry it a few feet so it wouldn't make noise. Then the stream narrowed and got deeper again so that I could float too. I felt Bill's paw and the wrapping was damp but not real wet, so I was happy that the bleeding had slowed. Bill slept right on because he'd had a busy day and knew I'd watch out for both of us.

I hadn't heard Hawkins yell for a long time. There wasn't anything for me to do but float and listen so I found the opener and got a can of beans. There wasn't a spoon so I ate with my fingers. It was pretty messy, but the creek was right there to wash my fingers in every few bites so it worked out all right.

Bullfrogs can make the air shake when they croak. And screech owls can just plain scare the fire out of me, even when I know it's coming. It was a loud noisy trip but Bill slept right through it all, which was the best thing he could do in his condition. I didn't wake him to see if he wanted some beans. Bill doesn't care much for beans all by themselves. But if there is some grease or gravy mixed in he'll eat them all and lick the bowl clean too.

37

Just a few minutes after first light I saw a piece of the bridge through the trees downstream. I was happy about it and looked into Bill's tub to see if he was awake yet. His eyes were still closed. I felt of his nose and it was dry and hot. There was a little puddle of blood in the bottom of the tub.

It was too deep to touch bottom, so I just had to wait for the current to float us down some more. I kicked a little and pushed water with my hands to get us toward the left side bank. I wondered which side Coy had been on when Dad floated through here and rang the bell.

The current drug us along slowly. There was a fallen tree trunk slanting down into the creek from the left and I decided to make for it so I could climb it out onto the bank when we got there. I kicked and hand-paddled because I was in a hurry now.

Something splashed into the water on the other side of the log and sent waves clear out to the middle. I stopped kicking but we drifted up against the log anyway.

Hawkins rose up from the water aside the log and yelled, "Surprise," just to scare me even worse. He had the nastiest smile a body could have. I screamed even though I didn't want to and he slapped me with his big rough hand.

"Surprise," he yelled, and slapped me again. "Where's the coins?" and another slap on the other side made a whistle noise inside my head.

"Here, take it, take it." I reached the treasure chest out of Bill's tub. Hawkins jerked it from me and slapped again, harder this time. The sound of his palm across my face was like a thunderclap and Bill came out of the tub in a snarling leap that took him right to Hawkins's neck.

Hawkins's eyes got big. Bill deep-growled and I heard the gristle snap in Hawkins's throat. Blood formed around Bill's side teeth. Hawkins swung the treasure box around to pound Bill's head. Bill's eyes were closed and his face had a look of deep contentment, like he was settled down for an evening of holding on, no matter what.

Hawkins grunted as he beat against Bill's head with the treasure box. He was the one most scared now because of the way Bill had him. He used both hands and his arm muscles stood out, but Bill kept his teeth buried deep. Hawkins beat at him again, and I knew it was hurting Bill really bad. I was screaming and hitting and scratching all the while too.

Hawkins hit Bill again, and I heard something crack that wasn't the box. Bill hung on, eyes still closed. I was still screaming and scratching. Hawkins slammed the box down again, then lost his balance and they were gone. I pushed off of my tube and followed them down.

I had to dive under twice to find them because they had stirred up a lot of sand. Hawkins's body was limp when I finally saw them, near the bottom, arms out to the side. Bill still had him at the neck. Blood and bubbles rose from Hawkins's face. His hair waved up from his head and wafted back and forth. I kicked myself down deeper and got a hold of Bill.

He couldn't hear me, but I talked in the water anyway. "Let go, Bill. Come on, let go now."

And he did let go, just in time, too, because I was running out of air. I gathered him up and kicked toward the top. I got a big breath and held Bill's head up. His eyes were shut and blood still dripped from his jaws. I yelled, "Bill," at him as I fought our way to the bank and laid him down into the weeds.

"Bill!"

He wasn't breathing. I pushed in on his chest a bunch of times and screamed his name and said,

"Please, God," and cried and gagged and swallowed. Then I picked him up by his hind legs and shook him up and down and a lot of water came out of his nose and mouth.

I laid him back down in the weeds and he still didn't breathe, so I held his mouth shut and blew in his nose holes. I tasted Hawkins's blood. I blew again, harder this time, and felt something give away. I blew again. It took this time and he made a little cough sound and more water came out.

"Come on, Bill." I could see his chest go up again by itself one time. I felt of it and could tell his heart was working now, too, and it was the best thing ever. I stayed there on my knees and quit crying so hard. Bill's eyes were still shut. I raised up an eyelid with my thumb and all there was was the white part.

I got Bill up in my arms and climbed the bank to the road. I had lost a shoe somewhere so I kicked off the other one and started running down the blacktop toward the town road. When I heard a car coming I turned around so they could see it was a girl carrying a hurt dog, but the man drove right on by. I hated him for it.

We ran some more and when I saw another car coming I got out in the middle so it had to stop or else run us over. His name was Ed because it said ED on the pocket of his shirt. He looked up at me through his car window.

"Please drive me to a doctor for my dog, Bill."

"I'm sorry but I'm going the other way and I'm—"

"You've got to."

"I'm late for work as it is."

I opened his back door and got in with Bill. Ed turned around and said, "Hey. Now look. You'll make me lose my job and it's—"

I looked down at Bill and said, "Please, please, please, please," and Ed tried to say something but I kept up with please, please, please, and pretty soon I felt the car moving.

Bill didn't move at all.

38

I was ashamed to not have any money to pay Dr. Hames for all he did. After he had felt Bill all over and listened with a thing that went in his ears, he made pictures of Bill's head with a machine. His wife helped, and put a neat white bandage on Bill's paw after she cleaned it and put yellow powder on it.

Dr. Hames was a big meaty man with black hair. He said, "Hmm," a lot and held up Bill's head pictures to a lighted box and studied them. The way he looked at me I knew he was going to say something worse than "Hmm."

"Multiple skull fractures." He made a face like the words hurt him to say.

Bill was on his side on top of the table. He didn't move at all unless I looked real close and saw his chest.

Doctor Hames said some other things about what was wrong with Bill. He used some words I had never heard before or read about.

"Will he wake up soon?"

He looked at his wife, then at me. "He might never wake up, Jess. You've got to know that. He might never wake up and if he does he probably won't be able to walk or even stand up. His brain has been badly damaged and, well, brains don't heal up like other tissues. When your brain gets damaged it's more or less permanent. He'd probably be blind, too, and deaf."

"Bill?"

"I'm sorry. It's a wonder he's still breathing."

"He's the best dog in the world."

"I know."

39

Mrs. Hames sat on the porch and we waited for Wrong Man to come get me and Bill in his car. Dr. Hames was tending to animals that folks had brought in to see him. Bill just laid there in the box with newspapers in the bottom and soft rags and a towel. I drank some tea Mrs. Hames fixed for me. It felt good to drink because it was hot, and I had been cold ever since the creek.

I remembered about my back pocket and felt inside of it. The creek water had turned the envelope into mush paper, but the coins were there, and the wedding band too. I gave a penny to Mrs. Hames.

"This is worth more than one cent because it's old," I told her. "Give it to the doctor for Bill, please."

She rubbed the penny between her fingers. "I'll see what he says."

Wrong Man drove up into the yard in his car. He was real worried looking and frowned. After I got sat down in the front seat he handed Bill in to me and put Bill's box in the backseat for later.

He drove slower than before. I told him all that happened since he drove me home yesterday.

It made him mad about what Hawkins had done. He asked me to go home and stay with him and Nell.

"When Bill wakes up he'll feel better if he sees that he's at home."

Wrong Man said, "Hmm," kind of like Dr. Hames.

"And besides, I have to see about Howard. He might be hurt pretty bad. He might even be dead or something."

"You think Hawkins is dead for sure?"

"Uh-huh. He was underwater and not moving."

"That sounds like dead all right. I'll have to tell the sheriff."

"It won't get Bill in trouble, will it?"

"No."

"So the box is gone?"

"Lost anyway."

40

When Dad first got out of jail he felt real sorry over what happened because he had got drunk and told Hawkins about the treasure. He never said he was sorry about it, but I knew that he was because he went to drinking whiskey even more than before, trying to forget.

It was the worst drinking he'd ever done, and part of it was my fault because I let him have the other three coins. Since Hawkins killed Howard, Dad said we needed to buy us another bull, but he spent it on store whiskey instead because he couldn't help himself. That kept him drunk a long time. He should have said he was sorry, though. At least once.

Bill had been asleep for eighty-three days when Wrong Man and Nell surprised me with a visit one morning. They told me it was Thanksgiving and they were on the way to spend the day with Nell's mother in Thomasville, but stopped first to see me and Bill. Dad was still in bed and feeling pretty bad. He had run out of whiskey and money both, and now his nerves were running fast on him.

Nell looked me over real good to see if I was eating enough and keeping clean. They came in to see Bill and patted him real easy and talked to him nice in quiet voices. We went back out on the porch and Nell said, "We would like you to come with us today if you could, Jess."

"That would be nice but I have to tend to Bill."

Wrong Man said, "Couldn't your dad look after him?"

"No."

"Has Bill moved at all? Wagged his tail or anything?"

"No, not yet."

Nell said, "We brought you some food. I don't know what got into me, Jess, but I cooked way too much of everything and wish you'd help me out and take some of it. I hate to throw it to the hogs."

I said that I would be glad to help and she made out like I was doing her a big favor, even though Nell knew that I knew all along that she fixed the food just for Bill and me in the first place. Wrong Man went out to the car and brought back four covered dishes.

We sat around some more and Wrong Man teased

me about Drury for a while, then he took out his watch and peered at it. "I suspect we best be getting on down the road, Nell."

Nell nodded and we all walked out into the front yard. I said, "Your car looks just like a new one, Wrong Man."

He said, "Not to brag or nothing, but I'm real easy on a car."

Nell looked at me and we smiled. Wrong Man mussed at my hair and Nell gave me a squeeze with both arms that I gave back to her before she got in the car. Nell likes me so much that it makes her cry when she leaves. I've never seen her cry but I can tell that she's going to because her chin gets all jabbered up.

Wrong Man said, "Nell's mother is baking pumpkin pies and she'll probably go and make too much. If she does, if there's a whole lot left over we might stop on the way back. Give you a piece or two."

"Okay."

"If we don't stop you'll know we ate it all."

"Okay."

Wrong Man started his car up and stuck his elbow out the window. His chin looked a little funny too. I said, "See you later, then."

"Only if there's too much pie," he said.

I said okay again because I knew there would be too much for sure and they would be back later. I waved them off and Wrong Man made his horn sound. Bill wasn't there to chase after them a ways.

BILL

There was turkey, dressing, gravy, and string beans. I cut a nice slice of white meat and put it on a plate. After I chopped it into little tiny pieces I added two spoons of gravy and mashed it all up together until it was like soup. Then I lifted Bill out of his bed and sat with him in the rocking chair by the stove. Bill had lost half of his size and I could hold him easy and light in my arms now.

I opened his mouth, then spooned in some food. It slid down his tongue toward his throat. The inside top of Bill's mouth has ridges in it, like a washboard. "It's turkey, Bill." His swallow muscles squeezed a little when it got way back there. "Nell brought it out just for you."

I closed his mouth for him and petted along his side. "Remember the last time you had Nell's turkey, Bill? It was at her house. Boy, I was mad at you for a while, taking everybody's napkin like you did, making me feed you some of her turkey before you'd turn loose. Remember that?"

I opened his mouth. The first bite had all gone down so I gave him another and let it slide. "That was kind of a bad thing to do, Bill, but it's sort of funny now to think back on it and remember. Real funny."

That bite went down clean too. "Wow, you like this turkey, don't you, buddy?" I dropped in another spoonful and rocked and remembered. "Bill, you sure were grand. There's just never been anyone could fetch a stick the way you could." I closed my eyes and rocked us slowly while we remembered it together. "The way you could turn and make the grass and dirt fly. Then you'd bring the stick back and hold your head up so high and proud and just grin."

I dropped in another bite for him. "And jump. Many a times I've watched you clear the fence like it was nothing at all. A sight to see."

I looked down at his sweet face. "You knew you were good, didn't you, Bill? You remember, don't you?"

I put down the plate and started working Bill's leg joints the way Dr. Hames had showed me, so that Bill wouldn't get all stiffened up. Dr. Hames said that one penny was worth so much that it paid for all the other times he came to see us and for the special food he brought too. The last time he was by and raised Bill's eyelid for a look some of the brown part was showing for the first time. I thought that was good and I think Dr. Hames thought so, too, but he said, "Chances are he'll never wake up again, Jess." I figured he just said that so I wouldn't get to counting on Bill being better. I don't think that one coin was worth all that much either.

I worked both his front legs like he was walking with them. Bill didn't move or make a sound but I knew that it felt good to him. I started on his back legs when Dad came in. He looked pretty rough. "Any coffee?"

"No. I'll make some in a few minutes, after I get done with Bill."

He sat with his elbows on the table so he could hold his head in both hands. "That dog is dead and don't know it. Wasting your time on that dog."

"Well, it's my time."

He turned his head a bit. "Don't be sassy."

I pushed Bill's eyelid up and saw there was even more brown than the last time. I said, "You're getting better. Every day you get a little better and this turkey will do you some good too."

Dad said, "That dog can't hear you."

"He hears more than you think."

"How about some coffee? Maybe some eggs, some soft-boiled eggs."

I worked Bill's tail around a few times before I laid him back in his box on his other side than before. I ground some beans and filled up the thing to where it said 6 CUPS. Then I put in four cups of water. "Go fetch some eggs if you want me to fix them."

"You mean you ain't fed the chickens yet?"

"No. We had company. Shaft Dudley and his wife came by. His first wife, Nell."

He pushed away from the table. "You tell Wrong Man anything?"

"About what?"

"Nothing." Dad stepped into his shoes and shuffled off to the chicken house. He was wrong when he said that Bill couldn't hear me. Even though he never moved I could tell that Bill was still in there some-where and that he heard me too.

I set some water on to boil. I wished now that I hadn't let Dad take those other three coins. I still had the wedding band and wore it around my neck on a braided leather necklace Wrong Man had fixed up for me good and strong so I wouldn't lose it.

Dad had got cold outside and was shaking more when he came back with the eggs. I dropped three into the pot where the water was steaming. Dad reached down a cup and was going to pour himself some coffee but when he lifted the pot it shook so much that I said, "Here, let me do that."

"You sure you got no more coins I can sell?"

"You got them all, Dad."

He had to use two hands to hold the cup steady. The water was starting to boil. "Do you want two eggs or three?"

"I need a few dollars is what I need. That's all, just a few dollars to buy some sugar and malt and yeast. Maybe a pint of whiskey to get settled down and I'll make a batch of blue john to sell and we'll be okay then."

"Well, there's no money that I know about." I took out the eggs with a spoon. "You want two eggs or three?"

"Wish we had a calf ready to sell."

I cracked and peeled two eggs for Dad and put down the bowl and a spoon in front of him on the table. He looked at them like eggs were something he'd never seen before.

I said, "Eat," and cracked the other egg for myself, because I wanted to save Nell's food for later when Dad was feeling better. Then we could eat together and talk about some things I wanted to tell him about his drinking.

Dad chopped his eggs up so that yellow mixed with the white. "There gas in the truck?"

I sat down next to him. "I don't know."

He ate two quick bites and swallowed without a chew. "I want you to give me that ring."

"Corbin's ring?"

"Yeah." He took another bite and drank his coffee.

"You can't have it."

"It ain't doing no good around your neck, so give me it." He stood up and knocked his chair back over.

I started to get up, too, but he pushed down on my shoulders and fingered the leather necklace. I said, "No," real loud and tucked my head down against the ring.

"Give me it."

"No." I tried to pull his hands from my shoulders but he was strong and leaning down.

Dad jerked the leather hard and it hurt my neck and burned at the skin. He jerked harder and I screamed, "Stop it," but Dad was crazy with it now and yanked terribly hard. The leather cut through my neck skin and I was screaming again so loud that I didn't hear it at first.

From across the room came a low mean growl, about the sweetest sound I ever heard. He was standing. It was Bill. He was back.

41

"Bill!"

Dad said, "Oh, God!"

Bill had stood up in his box. He was still growling low with his side teeth showing mean. His body was shaky but it was Bill standing up and awake and back from wherever he'd been to.

I was across the room, on my knees and holding him and saying, "Bill, oh Bill, oh Bill." The kitchen door slammed behind Dad as he stumbled out. Bill stopped growling and I just held him and it was so wonderful. Just me and Bill there on the floor and I was crying and happy and laughing and my tears got all over Bill's head and neck and he didn't mind because he was so glad to see me and I was so glad that he was back and I would never ask for anything more than just to be right there with Bill like that.

"I love you, Bill."

Bill loved me too. He wasn't strong enough to lick and show it, but I knew it anyway.

I heard Dad get his truck cranked and drive it past the house. I helped Bill try to walk and all he could do was small shaky steps because he would have to learn all over again after all those days asleep.

He drank some water and ate a little more turkey. But mostly he just wanted me to hold him and rock and talk to him, so I did. Later on he went to sleep, but not like before, and when he woke up we did some more walking. Six steps, which was pretty good.

I carried him outside and I could tell that he couldn't see out of his right eye, and just a little from the left. He smelled around and took some more little slow steps. I was so proud of him. He did a neat little job on the grass and tried to kick some dirt at it behind him but his legs wouldn't work for him.

"That's okay, Bill. Don't worry about it."

He got tired pretty quick and needed another nap. While he slept I got together my clothes and books and the pictures of Mom from the drawer.

When Bill woke up I had everything tied up in a bundle. He drank some more water and ate a little turkey. I talked to him and this time he wagged his tail some. It didn't wag very much, and only to one side, but it did wag a little and that was good enough for me.

Bill and I sat on the porch and he took the afternoon sun in his face to strengthen him. "Later on Wrong Man and Nell will come to see us, Bill. I think we should go live with them, if they still want us to. I think we'd do better, and I'd kind of like to try that school."

Bill gave it another little half wag.

"Wait until Dr. Hames sees you."

Just before the sun went down Wrong Man and Nell drove into the yard. They were happy about Bill too. We all cried and laughed and later, on the way to their house, Wrong Man sang a song for Bill called, "For he's a jolly good fellow, which nobody can deny." After I learned the words I sang it with him and so did Nell. Bill slept because he was tired from all the excitement, so we just sang it for each other, because we were all so glad about everything.

42

In the spring, when people started talking about how it was the worst dry spell anybody remembered and how wells were going dry and creeks running low, I got to thinking and planning.

The day after school let out Nell and I fixed a big picnic lunch and packed a basket with fried chicken, potato salad, biscuits, and a Thermos of iced tea.

Nell rode in the front with Wrong Man and Drury and I sat in the back with Bill and that bird dog that Wrong Man had traded Carl Etter out of. He had named him Knife so people would ask about such an unusual name and he could tell the trading story all over again. He still wasn't tired of it and I still liked it too.

When we parked at the Sandtown Road bridge I

got scary feelings and had to swallow lots of times. The water was way down from the drought, just like folks had said.

We walked under the bridge. Wrong Man and Drury took off their shirts and shoes. Nell and I took off our dresses because we had bathing suits underneath from a store. Drury looked at me more than ever. My body had changed some. I didn't look as fullsome as my mom did in those pictures, but I wasn't straight up and down anymore either.

Wrong Man said, "Close your mouth, Drury."

I told Bill to stay and guard our food until we got back. I was afraid that he wasn't strong enough to swim, even with the creek down. Bill was still very slow moving. He was blind in one eye and didn't see much out of the other. His hearing was weak unless you hollered. Dr. Hames said it was already a miracle and that he probably wouldn't get much better and that was all right. Deep inside of himself Bill was as good as ever.

The four of us went in the creek together and held hands for balance so we could feel along the bottom with our feet. Knife ran along the bank most of the time with his nose to the ground. I had never held a boy's hand before.

In the second pool downstream from the bridge my foot came up against something square feeling and I told everybody to stop. The water was only up to my belly button but I had to go under twice to pull it out of the sand. I could tell that it was old man Corbin's box and the screwdriver was still there, holding the lid shut down tight. I let just my head come out first, then I raised out the box and held it high and said, "Heh, heh, heh."

Everybody laughed and yelled and danced in the water. I handed the box to Wrong Man, then I hugged Nell, and then hugged Drury, which surprised him. It surprised me, too, the way it happened so fast. We stepped back and looked at one another.

Wrong Man said, "This chest is surely heavy."

Drury was still looking at me and I was looking back at him. I said, "Would you call me Jessica from now on?"

"Sure."

I started pushing back upstream through the water as hard as I could. Wrong Man said, "Where you going, Jess?"

"Back to the bridge," I said. "Come on."

Drury said, "Call her Jessica."

Wrong Man said, "What for?"

I climbed out onto the bank and started running. Bill was sitting under the bridge next to our basket of food. He's a very good guard. "Hey, Bill," I hollered.

He turned his head sideways so he could watch me coming with his one good eye. I scrambled up the slope, dropped down on my knees by him, all out of breath. I gave him a good hug. "We found it again."

ABOUT THE AUTHOR

Herbert Reaver, known to his friends as Chap, was a chiropractor in Marietta, Georgia. He was the author of two other novels for Delacorte Press, *Mote* and *A Little Bit Dead*, both winners of the Edgar Award for Best Young Adult Mystery. Chap Reaver died in January 1993. He is survived by his wife, Dixie, and two grown sons.